Do ghosts talk on-line?

Who are you? I typed.

Friends. We're friends.

No, you're not our friends! I pounded into the keyboard.

Came to warn you.

The message disappeared, and the whole screen was covered with a jumble of letters. It looked like alphabet soup.

"It's messed up," Jeff said in disgust. "Dad must have hooked it up wrong. Either that or the whole system has crashed!"

"Or someone decided to mess around with our screen," I said indignantly.

I typed in *Who are you?* again.

For a moment, nothing happened. Then most of the letters vanished, leaving only a few letters dancing across the screen. *"G-H-O-S-T-W-E-B,"* I read aloud. "Ghostweb?"

The computer let out a high screeching sound, and the screen went blank.

CYBER ZONE

Visitor from the Beyond

CYBER ZONE

Visitor from the Beyond

S. F. Black

Troll

Art direction by Fabia Wargin.
Cover art by Peter Scanlan.

Printed in the United States of America.

10 9 8 7 6 5 4 3 2

Chapter 1

"Okay, Amanda," my mom puffed as she shoved aside a huge empty crate. "We've made a good start in here. Now why don't you find Jeff and start unpacking the boxes in the kitchen?"

I glanced around the room—our new living room. I couldn't imagine what Mom meant by a good start. There were boxes everywhere. In fact, the whole place looked like a major hurricane just hit it. As I stood up, a cloud of dust rose around my feet. I looked down at myself and groaned. My pink denim overalls were covered with dirty smudges.

"I know, it's awful," Mom said, giving me a sympathetic look. "I always forget how much work moving is."

"Yeah, well, maybe if you'd remembered, we wouldn't have had to move," I muttered.

Mom raked her hands through her short, sleek brown hair. "Come on, Amanda. It's not that bad. Once we get moved in and adjusted, I bet you'll really like it here. Look at how much room we have!"

I looked around unenthusiastically. Our new house did have a ton of room, but it was also old, creepy-looking, and in the middle of nowhere. I thought longingly of our apartment in New York City. Maybe it was cramped, but at least it was cozy.

Mom gestured at the fireplace. "And we certainly never had a fireplace in our apartment in New York!"

"So?" I retorted. I glanced up at the dusty oil painting of Great-Aunt Libby hanging above the fireplace. She looked like a nice old lady. She was wearing a long print dress, and her white hair was pinned up in a bun. Nevertheless, I scowled at her. *If you hadn't died and left Dad this house,* I told her picture silently, *we never would have come here!*

No matter how hard I tried, I couldn't believe my parents had decided to move here. *Here* was Haneytown, New Hampshire. If you've never heard of it, don't worry. I'd never heard of it, either, until my dad's great-aunt Libby left him her old farmhouse, and my dad and mom decided to move us all here. My dad always wanted to live in the country, but my mom grew up in the city just like me. Plus she worked as a restaurant reviewer for the *Daily News*. That's why I was sure she'd talk Dad out of the idea of moving to Great-Aunt Libby's old farm. After all, how many restaurants could there be in a tiny place like Haneytown? But instead, she went right along with him. "I've wanted to retire and write a cookbook for years," she had gushed. "Here's my chance. Besides, living in the country will be so much healthier for you and Jeff. Fresh air, open spaces, good schools . . ."

The only problem was that I loved the city. I loved the subways, the crowds, all the different restaurants, the museums, and most of all, the stores. I also loved my school, Saint Hilda's—even if the building was sort of falling apart. New York was noisy and inconvenient just like my mom and dad said, but at least it was fun and exciting. As far as I could tell, living in the country was going to be dull, dull, dull!

What I was thinking must have showed on my face, because Mom reached out and gave me a hug. "Amanda, I promise it's not going to be that bad," she said quietly. "This is a wonderful old house."

"A wonderful old haunted house," I corrected bitterly. I didn't really believe it was haunted, but Dad had joked that Great-Aunt Libby once warned him there were ghosts here.

"Amanda, that's just silly," Mom said sharply. "Look," she continued, her voice softening, "I know it isn't easy starting over someplace new, especially when you're twelve, but you have to think of it as gaining something rather than losing something. You'll still be able to visit the city, Amanda, only you'll have the new experience of living in the country."

"What about all my friends?" I demanded.

"You'll make new friends," Mom said.

"Right, a bunch of country kids who've never been anywhere and don't know anything and dress funny!"

My mom's eyes flashed. "Amanda, stop it. You're being prejudiced. You can't judge a person by where they grew up or how they look. You know better than that."

I blushed, guilty as charged. "I guess," I said. "I'm sorry. I'm just really going to miss my old friends. I can't believe I won't have Tara and Marriane anymore!"

"You'll still have Tara and Marriane, Amanda," Mom said in an annoyed tone. "Your dad's upstairs hooking up your computer right now. I insisted he do that before he moved the furniture inside so I wouldn't have to listen to your whining about living in the sticks. In an hour you should be able to go on-line and talk to the Sixth Grade Supers."

I groaned. "Not *Supers*, Mom. *Superstars!*"

"Whatever." Mom grinned at me.

I didn't grin back. She and my dad thought that talking to my friends on the Net would be the same as being back in the city with them, but I knew it wouldn't work that way. Tara and Marriane would be together and I'd be stuck out here, alone, in the middle of nowhere. I swallowed.

"Well, I guess I'd better go find Jeff," I mumbled.

"Yeah. Where is he?" Mom asked.

"He's probably just trying to weasel out of work, as usual," I said crossly. "Hey, Jeff," I shouted, clomping out into the hallway. "Jeeeff! Where are you?"

There was no answer.

Figures, I thought resentfully. Jeff and I usually got along pretty well, even though he's three years younger than me, but today my brother was really getting on my nerves. Besides not helping one bit, he was starting to act all excited about our new house. At first, he'd been as upset about moving as I was, but now he was starting to say stuff like "Isn't this house cool, Amanda?" and "The country is really kind of awesome!"

I stomped into the kitchen and started tearing open a taped-up box of dishes. "Hey, Jeff!" I bellowed. "Time to get to work. Get out here. Now!"

I wasn't expecting any response, but all of a sudden I heard footsteps behind me. "Jeff?" I whirled around. Then I gasped.

A white-clad figure covered in cobwebs and black soot was lurching toward me from an alcove behind the old-fashioned refrigerator. It looked like a ghost!

I stepped backward, my heart thudding.

"Wh-who are you?" I yelped.

Chapter 2

The figure under the sheet let out a squeal of laughter.

I felt my cheeks get hot. "Jeff!" I shrieked, lunging toward him. "You little creep. You almost gave me a heart attack!"

Jeff's head poked out from the corner of the sheet. His face was streaked with black. It looked like he'd been climbing down a chimney. I wrinkled up my nose. "Yech! You smell like an old fire," I said. "Where were you, anyway? I've been working my brains out, and you're supposed to be helping!"

Jeff grinned. Even if he weren't my little brother, I'd have to admit he's a cute kid. He has reddish, curly hair, bright blue eyes, and a ton of freckles. And when he smiles, his mouth turns up in this funny, crooked way. When Jeff was a baby he won a prize at our community center for having the cutest grin. He's never forgotten it, either. He uses that grin all the time to get his way. "You're not going to believe it, Amanda. I found a secret door!"

"What? Where?" I asked.

"Here." Jeff swung the door of the alcove shut. I blinked. He was right. When the door was shut, you couldn't even tell it was there. In spite of myself, I felt excited. Having a secret door in your own house could be kind of neat. But I was still mad at Jeff for scaring me.

"So?" I said coolly. "Big deal. In an old farmhouse like this, there are probably tons of secret doors. Only they all just lead into closets."

Jeff's blue eyes glimmered. "This one doesn't." He leaned toward me. "It leads up to the attic," he whispered. "Come on. I'll show you."

"Okay," I replied cautiously.

"But shhh!" Jeff held his finger to his lips. "We don't want Dad and Mom to find out about this."

I nodded and followed him through the narrow doorway. Once we were inside, Jeff silently pulled the secret door shut behind us. When I heard the click of the lock, I jumped. "What if we get trapped in here?" I said with a frown.

"No sweat. We can always take the main staircase out," Jeff replied.

I peered around. It was dark, but there was some light from a tiny round window far above us—enough light that I could see a flight of crooked stairs rising up. The walls looked mostly black, but here and there I could see patches of old-fashioned wallpaper covered with faded pink roses. Suddenly I caught my breath. The walls were mostly black because they'd been burned. So had the wooden stair treads. It looked as if the whole passage had been swallowed up in flames!

"Wow," I said, climbing lightly up the stairs after my little brother. "There must have been a really bad fire here."

"There was," Jeff said.

"What are you talking about?" I hissed.

"Didn't Dad tell you?"

12

We stepped up into a wide, low attic. The thick roof timbers had scorch marks on them, too.

"Tell me what?"

"About sixty-five years ago, the top floor of the house caught fire," Jeff said in a solemn voice. "The family that was living here—I think it was Great-Aunt Libby's brother's family—all died in the fire."

Now I did remember Dad mentioning something about a fire, but I hadn't paid much attention. "That's horrible!" I said.

"Yeah," my brother agreed.

"How did the fire start?"

"I don't know." Jeff shrugged. "That's all Dad told me."

I glanced around. The corner of the attic we were standing in was piled with stuff—junk mostly. A bunched-up tablecloth embroidered with a picture of bluebirds and strawberries lay at my feet. "Pretty," I said. Then I noticed one side of it was burned. I bent over and picked it up. A rustling sound filled the air as something fell out. Pieces of paper fluttered around me. They were old photographs. I reached out and grabbed one in midair.

Jeff peered over my shoulder as I held it up to the light of the small window. "Cool," he said. "Check it out. They're kids like us."

I stared at the picture. A boy and a girl were sitting on some steps side by side. The girl was rolling her eyes and twisting up her mouth in a way that was so familiar, I smiled to myself. I knew that face. Her little brother was driving her nuts! It was the same face I made whenever Jeff was being especially annoying. Then I looked at the boy. It was hard to tell in a black-and-white photo, but it looked as if he had red hair like Jeff. In fact, except that he was wearing a pair of old-fashioned-looking knickers, a white shirt with long sleeves, and a bow tie, he looked a lot like my little brother. I squinted at the girl, trying to see if she looked like me, but she didn't really. Her hair was blonde and wavy, while mine is dark brown and straight. Still, the expression on her face reminded me of myself.

"I wonder who they are—or were," I said softly.

"Don't you know?" Jeff's voice sounded funny. "They're the kids who died in the fire. It hurt them a lot. They screamed and screamed but no one came. They were locked in."

I stared at my brother. His eyes were shut, and he was rocking to and fro.

"Jeff, stop it," I exclaimed. "Don't scare me like that, okay? Stop it!" I reached out and shook him hard. His eyes opened, and he grinned up at me.

"Jeff, I can't believe you're being such a jerk!"

"Huh?" my brother said.

I scowled at him. "I can't believe you'd say something so gruesome about these kids," I burst out.

Jeff frowned. "Who are they?" he asked, gazing at the picture wonderingly.

I gaped at him. "Jeff, you just told me who they are. The kids who died in the fire!"

"That's really awful," my brother said slowly.

I gave him a look. "Jeff, is this some kind of joke?"

"What are you talking about?" He sounded genuinely confused.

I stared at him hard. "Don't you remember what you just said?"

Jeff shook his head.

An icy tremor ran up my spine.

"I did feel kind of weird just now," my brother added in a puzzled voice.

"What do you mean?"

"I don't know. I got dizzy for a minute, and the next thing I knew you were staring at me with a funny look on your face."

I sucked in my breath. If my little brother was trying to scare me, it was working. But if he wasn't . . . I stuffed the picture into the front pocket of my overalls.

Just then I heard my dad's voice.

"Jeff! Amanda!" he was yelling. "Come here right away!"

Chapter 3

Jeff and I took off so fast that we almost tumbled down the narrow staircase. We slipped out through the secret door into the kitchen, breathing hard.

Dad was standing by the kitchen table. "Hey, where'd you guys pop out from?" he exclaimed when he saw us.

"Uhh, we were just exploring," Jeff said quickly. I could tell he was trying to keep the secret door a secret, but it was no use. Dad had to have seen us come out of there.

A smile spread over my dad's face. "You found the secret door, huh?" he asked. "I thought that was the greatest thing when I was a boy." My dad's face became serious. "But listen, kids, you have to promise me never to go in there again—"

"But Dad—" Jeff protested.

"Listen to me. That staircase isn't stable. It was never rebuilt after the fire. And there's an old well shaft beneath it. If you fell through the floor or the wall, you could be killed. Is that understood?"

Jeff didn't say anything.

"Sure, I understand," I said. In a way I was sort of relieved we weren't allowed to go in there. The burned staircase and the attic were both pretty spooky.

"Jeff?" Dad and my brother locked eyes for a few seconds.

"Okay, I won't go in there anymore," Jeff said sullenly.

"Great." A smile slid over my Dad's face. "Now for the good news," he said triumphantly. "I've hooked you up, Amanda. Come on up to your room. Your friends are waiting to say hi!"

I smiled, too. "Tara and Marriane are on-line?" I exclaimed. "Awesome! How'd you get hold of them so quickly?"

My dad looked sheepish. "I'm not exactly sure. All I know is I turned on the modem and there they were!"

"Is Mouse there, too?" Jeff squealed. Mouse is Tara's little brother, Morris. Everyone calls him Mouse because he looks sort of like a little gray mouse: skinny with big ears and big eyes. He's Jeff's best friend, and Tara, Marriane, and I let the two of them use our chat room, mostly so they won't bug us when we're talking.

"I don't know. Why don't you come up and find out for yourself?" Jeff and I ran up the stairs. My dad's a graphic artist and does a lot of work on the computer. Still, I hadn't expected him to to get me on-line so quickly.

I ran into my new bedroom and pulled a chair up to my computer desk. A message was on the screen. *Hello, Amanda and Jeff.* I frowned. Usually, Tara would use our on-line names. An on-line name is like a nickname you use on the Net. Mine is *Banana,* because it rhymes with Amanda, and when I was a little kid bananas were my favorite food. Jeff's is *Monster* because he loves monster movies.

I glanced at the return address. But instead of *RealGirl* or *Madeline*—Tara's and Marriane's on-line names—there was just a bunch of numbers, letters, and symbols I didn't recognize.

"$$%ffgggzzzttt," I read aloud. Then I chuckled. Tara and Marriane were probably so excited to talk to me that they'd accessed the chat room wrong or something.

Hey, RealGirl, or is it Madeline? I typed in. *How are you doing?* Tara picked *RealGirl* for her on-line name because she's really into girl stuff like clothes and make-up, but she's tough, too, and she thought RealGirl sounded sort of like Wonder Woman. Marriane's is *Madeline* because she wants to be an actress when she grows up, and she thinks Madeline sounds mysterious and glamorous— much more like a name for a famous actress than plain old Marriane.

RealGirl. Pretty good. How are you?

Not too bad, I typed. Then I paused. I'd been dying to get on-line and talk to my friends, but now I wasn't sure what to say. Before, we'd always talked about what we were going to do that weekend or what had happened at school that day, like the weird outfits people had worn or who had a crush on whom in our class. We could still talk about that stuff, but it wouldn't be the same with me out in Nowheresville. *So did you hit the sale at Bloomingdale's yet?* I typed.

Bloomingdale's? Tara wrote back.

I grinned. Tara likes to pretend she isn't into shopping, but that's a major lie. The girl is definitely in the running for shopaholic of all time. Of course, she plans to be a fashion designer when she grows up, so it makes sense.

Yeah, sure, you never heard of Bloomingdale's, I typed, *and I'm Amanda-Banana, Queen of the Jungle.*

You are? Tara said.

I frowned. Tara didn't seem like herself, but then she probably felt just as strange as I did. We'd been best friends since third grade. We'd always done everything together, and now we were hundreds of miles away from each other.

I blinked as another message appeared on the screen. *Amanda, Amanda and Jeff! Hello, hello!*

I checked the return address. *Gggh%%sss@$W995!#.* More gibberish! *Hello, who's this?* I wrote, frowning. It had to be Marriane, or maybe Mouse, whose on-line name was *Mickey*.

It's—the screen blinked—*Marriane.*

Hi, Marriane. I wondered why she wasn't using her on-line name. Marriane loves the name Madeline. Sometimes she even makes us call her Madeline at school.

So what's going on there? It was Tara again.

Nothing. Well, not nothing. Jeff and I found a secret door in the kitchen. It leads to a staircase that goes to the attic. There was a fire here a long time ago, and the staircase was sealed up. It's creepy. The fire was really bad and the family that used to live here—

I was about to type *died* when the phone rang. The noise made me jump. I heard Mom pick it up out in the hall. "Amanda," she called, "it's for you! Hurry up. It's long distance."

Hang on. I have to go for a minute, I typed into the computer as fast as I could. Then I sped down the hall.

Mom held the phone out to me. "It's Tara," she hissed.

"Tara?" I mouthed back in surprise. I pulled the receiver to my ear. "Tara?" I said.

"I couldn't wait to call you!" Tara's familiar voice burbled. "I tried to get you on-line, but I guess you're not hooked up yet. I miss you already. Mom and I went to the sale at Bloomingdale's today and got you the greatest dress. It's short and it's plaid—plaid is totally in right now—and—"

"Tara!" I blurted. "Why are you calling? I was just talking to you on-line."

"What?"

"When you called I was in the *Superstars* chat room, talking to you."

"Amanda, are you nuts?" Tara demanded. "Marriane and I are sitting right here in my room. We just had the computer on, but you weren't there, so we turned it off again."

"But—"

"It must be somebody playing a joke."

"I guess so," I said weakly. "Maybe Mouse got on-line and pretended to be you."

"Nope," Tara said. "Mouse has soccer practice today. Right now he's in Central Park with a million other screaming little soccer fanatics."

"That's funny."

"It's probably some weirdo. All kinds of strange people get on-line."

"But how did they know our on-line names?" I asked softly.

Tara didn't hear me, or if she did, she didn't know what to say. "Well, I had to call to say hi, but I can't stay on very long. It's long distance, unfortunately. Here, hold on. Marriane wants to say hello."

Marriane's voice came on the line. "Amanda, how are you? Did you meet any cute boys yet?" she chirped. Marriane is really nice and very smart. She also happens to be totally boy crazy.

I sighed. "Are you kidding? I just got here. I haven't met anyone yet."

"Tara and I want to come up and visit you over summer vacation. We really miss you, Amanda. We've decided to wear nothing but black all week. Here, I'm going to put Tara back on."

There was a burst of static, and I could hear Tara's mom's voice in the background. "Time to get off, Tara. It's silly to waste money for a phone call when you can talk on the Net."

"But Mom!" Tara wailed. "All right. Hey, Amanda," she said into the receiver. "Listen, I have to go. I'll send you the dress I got you. Make sure your dad hooks you up soon, okay? That way we can talk as much as we want."

"Okay. Bye, Tara. Bye, Marriane," I said and hung up the phone. My heart was pounding triple-time. If I hadn't been talking to Tara and Marriane in the chat room, who had I been talking to?

I sprinted back down the hall. The door to my room was open a crack, and inside I could hear the faint buzz of the computer. I burst through the door.

"Hey!" Jeff whirled around. "You scared me!"

"What are you doing at my computer?" I demanded.

"Dad hasn't hooked mine up yet!" Jeff protested.

"Who are you talking to?"

Jeff looked at me like I was crazy. "Mouse, of course. Why?"

I nudged him aside and crouched down in front of the keyboard. *You are not Mouse,* I typed. *Who are you?*

"Amanda, what are you doing?"

"Mouse has soccer practice today," I replied grimly. "That was Tara and Marriane on the phone. They said they tried to get us, and we weren't hooked up yet!"

Jeff's mouth fell open. "You mean someone is pretending to be Mouse?" he cried in disbelief.

Who are you? I typed in again.

Friends. We're friends.

No, you're not our friends! I pounded into the keyboard.

Came to warn you.

"Hey!" Jeff yelped. "Amanda, look!" He pointed at the corner of the screen where the clock was. "It's moving."

I sucked in my breath. The clock *was* moving, only it wasn't moving forward. It was moving backward.

"What's going on?" I breathed.

The clock stopped, and a new date appeared in the upper left-hand corner: 06-07-32. "Six-seven-thirty-two," I read aloud. "I don't get it."

I glanced down at the main screen again. The message had disappeared, and the whole screen was covered with a jumble of letters. It looked like alphabet soup.

"It's messed up," Jeff said in disgust. "Dad must have hooked it up wrong. Either that or the whole system has crashed!"

"Or whoever is playing a joke on us decided to mess around with our screen," I said indignantly.

I typed in *Who are you?* again.

For a moment, nothing happened. Then most of the letters vanished, leaving only a few letters dancing across the screen. *"G-H-O-S-T-W-E-B,"* I read aloud. "Ghostweb?"

The computer let out a high screeching sound, and the screen went blank.

"Dad!" Jeff shouted.

Dad poked his head into the room. "What's up?"

"You've got to look at Amanda's computer again. It's not working right."

My dad walked over to my computer table. "What's wrong with it? It looks like you guys just turned it off."

"No, we didn't," Jeff said dully. "It went off by itself."

"Don't be ridiculous." My dad leaned over me and hit the start button. The computer buzzed, but the screen remained blank.

My dad clicked the reset button a couple of times. "I don't get it," he said. "It should be working. I'll have to check the phone line."

He turned to me. "Amanda, you don't mind hanging on a few more hours, do you? I'd like to make sure the movers get the rest of the furniture into the house before I fix your computer. It looks like it's about to rain, and your mom will kill me if the couch gets soaked."

"No, that's cool," I replied shakily.

"Great." My dad headed out the door.

Jeff and I stared at each other.

"Jeff," I whispered. "Who do you think we were talking to?"

"Well, they said they were ghosts, right?" Jeff whispered back.

A shiver went up my spine. "Jeff, you don't really believe that, do you?" I asked softly.

"Yes, I do," my brother replied. "They're ghosts and they're coming to get us!"

"Jeff, stop it!" I shrieked.

Then I saw the corners of his mouth twitch. "Gosh, Amanda," he wheezed, cackling like a lunatic. "You should see your face. You look like you're about to faint. Don't tell me you believe in ghosts!"

"Oh, shut up," I snapped. "Of course I don't. But if they weren't ghosts, who were those people we were talking to?"

Jeff shrugged. "Who knows? Probably just kids in some other chat room. Dad hooked you up, right? You know how absentminded he is. He probably got the address wrong and thought he was in the right chat room. When we started talking, the kids in the other chat room just went along with it."

I looked at my brother in surprise. For a little twerp, he was pretty smart. Jeff's explanation made sense. For one thing, it explained why the person I thought was Tara had been so clueless when I asked her about Bloomingdale's.

"It's possible," I admitted grudgingly.

"It's what happened," Jeff declared. "Now all we have to do is make sure Dad hooks us up right next time."

I nodded, but something still bothered me. If a bunch of kids were just playing a joke, how did they know our real names?

Chapter 4

"**M**ore mashed potatoes, anyone?" Dad asked sleepily.

We were all sitting around the kitchen table. Mom had cooked a big dinner because she said she'd wanted our first night in our new house to be special. She'd made roast chicken with bread stuffing and her special garlic mashed potatoes. If you like garlic—and I do—they're the best. The meal was delicious, like everything my mom cooks, but I could hardly taste any of it. I couldn't stop thinking about the fire. It gave me the creeps, even though it had happened so long ago. What had happened with my computer gave me the creeps, too. Maybe someone had just been playing a joke on us. But who? And why?

I jumped as a clap of thunder made the windows rattle. It had been raining and thundering since four o'clock. Dad said it was pretty normal to get big thunderstorms like this in the mountains, but it still freaked me out.

What if a lightning bolt started the fire? I thought.

I cleared my throat. "Uh, Dad?"

"Yes, sweetheart?"

"You know the fire that happened here a long time ago? Did Great-Aunt Libby's brother's family really die?"

My dad's face turned solemn. "I'm afraid so. My great-uncle and his wife and kids all died of smoke inhalation."

"How did the fire start?" I asked.

"Yeah," said Jeff. "What happened exactly?"

"I don't really know," Dad replied quickly. "It was a long time ago, and—"

"There's no point in dredging up old tragedies," Mom cut in. She pushed her empty plate away. "Besides, it's getting late, and you two have your first day of school tomorrow."

"Mom, it's not that late!" I wailed.

"It is for the country," my dad said, winking at me. "Your mother's right. It's been a long day, and it's way past bedtime for all of us. Are you finished with your dinner, Amanda?"

"I guess so," I mumbled, getting up from my chair.

"Then up to bed! You, too, Jeff."

I hesitated. It had been a long day, but I didn't exactly feel like going to bed. Plus, it wasn't like Mom and Dad to rush us off to bed like this. It also wasn't like them to not answer our questions.

Jeff drained the last of his milk and stood up. "Is that who Great-Aunt Libby thought was haunting the house?" he demanded. "Great-Uncle Arthur and his family—the people who died in the fire?"

Mom sighed. "Jeff, don't be absurd," she said. "There are no ghosts in this house!"

At that moment another thunderbolt resounded nearby and the lightbulb overhead flickered. Jeff's eyes went wide and so did mine.

Dad chuckled. "Well, Maureen, I guess the ghost that doesn't exist wants to make sure to let us know he's there!"

"Dan, that's not funny!" my mom declared. "There are no such things as ghosts."

"So why did Great-Aunt Libby think the house was haunted?" I said.

"Libby was in her nineties when she died," Mom answered slowly. "She believed in a lot of old-time country superstitions." She gathered our plates in a stack and stood up. "Now, for the last time, you two get to bed or you'll never be up in time for school."

Jeff and I exchanged a glance. Then, reluctantly, we walked out of the kitchen and trudged upstairs. "Boy, did you notice how strange Mom and Dad were acting?" Jeff whispered as we opened a box on the bathroom floor to look for our toothbrushes. "I wonder why they don't want to talk about the fire."

"Well, it is a creepy story," I whispered back as I pulled my toothbrush and a new tube of toothpaste out of the bottom of the box. "Maybe they don't want to talk about it because they're worried it'll make us not like it here."

Jeff relaxed. "You're probably right," he said. "Well, good-night, Amanda-Banana."

"Good-night, Monkey." Usually my brother hated it when I called him Monkey. It was his family nickname as a really little kid, because he loved to climb things, but lately he had been saying it sounded like a baby name. Tonight he just smiled and padded down the hall.

I finished brushing my teeth, went to my room, and pulled on my nightgown. Switching off my bedside lamp, I crawled into bed. My new room was about three times the size of my old one. I could remember when I'd wanted a big room more than anything, but now, lying there in the dark, my new room felt way too big. *Big and spooky, just like the rest of this house,* I thought nervously.

I looked out the window just as a bolt of lightning lit up the sky. It looked like a wild burst of flame. *That had to be how the fire started,* I thought with a shiver. *A bolt of lightning!* I pulled my covers up around my chin and curled up in a tight ball, wondering how I'd ever get to sleep. However, a few minutes later, I felt a heaviness steal over my body as my eyes slowly closed.

The next thing I knew, I heard a noise somewhere close by. I opened my eyes and peered out the window. The rain had stopped, and the moon was shining round and bright, giving the room an eerie greenish glow. I sat up in bed. Then I caught my breath. The greenish glow wasn't from the moon. It was from my computer. The machine was on!

I stared at it, rubbed my eyes, and stared again.

A message was on the screen. Slipping out of bed, I tiptoed across the creaky wooden floor.

Came to warn you! the message read.

Still groggy, I leaned over the keyboard and typed.

Warn me of what?

Danger. Don't play with matches, flashed the reply. *Be careful, Amanda, Jeff. Be very careful.*

I felt as if I'd been struck by a bolt of lightning. I stretched my hands over the keyboard, but they were shaking so much that I couldn't punch the keys.

"Who are you?" I said. My voice sounded so loud that it startled me. I took a deep breath, trying to calm myself down. That was when I smelled something burning. Looking up, I noticed the room was rapidly filling with smoke!

I took another breath, then began to cough. Something was burning, burning, burning! It hurt my lungs even to breathe!

Leaping to my feet, I shouted, "Help! Fire! Fire!"

I turned and ran for the door, but it was engulfed in flames. Standing in the scorching fire was a girl—the girl from the photograph! I blinked. I had to be imagining it, but she was standing right there, real as life, and she was smiling.

"Amanda," she said in a high, whispery voice. "I'm so glad you've come." I tried to back away, but she reached out her hand and grabbed me. Suddenly I realized what she was doing. She was pulling me into the fire!

"Let go!" I screamed. "Let me go!" I struggled to pull back, but she only tugged me closer and closer. I could feel the heat of the flames spreading over my body, singeing my hair, my skin. "Please, let go!" I pleaded.

I lifted my head, but the girl was gone. There was only a hand—no, it was an inhuman claw—pinning me down, making sure I could never escape. I heard mocking laughter, and suddenly I glimpsed a pair of yellow, glowing eyes boring into mine. Out of the smoke a face emerged. It looked like a Halloween monster mask, wrinkled and green, a goblin face grinning evilly at me through the flames.

Chapter 5

"**A**manda, wake up! You're having a bad dream!"

I opened my eyes. There was no smoke, no flames, no goblin leering at me—just Mom leaning over my bed, gently shaking my shoulders.

"I thought . . . the house was burning!" I croaked.

Mom's eyes darkened. "The story about that old fire really scared you, huh?" she said anxiously. "Well, don't worry, honey. You're right here and everything's fine. In fact, it's a gorgeous morning!"

I lifted my head. The window was open wide, and bright sunlight was streaming through the curtains. I sniffed. The air smelled of green grass and flowers, and . . . something burning!

I sat up fast. "Mom, something *is* burning!" I cried.

"Oh, no! My pancakes," Mom moaned. "Hurry and get dressed," she called as she dashed out of the room. "You have only forty-five minutes to catch the school bus."

I groaned, dreading the thought of going to school and not knowing a single person. My new school? I never wanted to leave my old one. But I forced myself out of bed and pulled on a pale pink T-shirt and a pair of white jeans. Not very adventurous fashionwise, but I had a feeling my new school wasn't exactly going to be the fashion capital of the universe.

When I got downstairs, Mom was standing at the stove fanning the smoke away from a skillet of blackened pancakes. "Oh, dear!" she exclaimed. "I was sure I turned the burner off."

"Maybe Great-Aunt Libby's ghost turned it back on," Jeff suggested from the table.

Mom waved her spatula at him. "Yeah, right, Mr. Wise Guy. Now what are we going to do about breakfast? I don't have time to make more batter."

"We can have Loopy Loops," Jeff said eagerly.

"Loopy Loops?" Mom sniffed. "Those things are stuffed with sugar." Maybe because she's so into cooking, Mom hates it when we eat junk food. She keeps only one box of sugared cereal, for emergencies like this one.

"Please?" Jeff pleaded.

Mom's face softened into a smile. "Okay, just this once."

Jeff poured himself a giant-sized bowl. "Want some, Amanda?"

"No, thanks, I'll just have a piece of toast," I murmured. My head felt funny—smoggy—like I really had inhaled lungsful of burning smoke. I shivered, remembering my dream—the flames, the girl from the photograph, and most of all the strange creature who had tried to keep me in the flames. It had all seemed so real.

I crunched down a mouthful of dry toast.

Dad walked into the kitchen and glanced at the clock on the wall.

"Better hurry, kids," he said cheerfully. "It's a half-mile walk to the school bus."

31

Jeff looked horrified. "You're kidding, right?"

My dad grinned. "No, but cheer up. It'll be good for you. Build up those muscles of yours."

"But I don't want big muscles," Jeff complained. He looked at me and made a face. I made a face back. Ever since my parents had decided to move to the country, Mom and Dad had been going on about how life in the city had made us both weaklings, and how from now on we were both going to get a lot more fresh air and exercise. The only catch was that I hated exercise!

Still, I slung my new backpack—the one that said *I Love New York* on it—over my shoulder and started for the door. Jeff gulped down the milk in the bottom of his bowl and trotted after me.

It felt funny to walk out our front door into a big green field. Funny, but sort of nice, too.

We headed down the dirt driveway past a crowd of little brown birds pecking at the ground. At the gate, we had to duck under a big lilac bush covered with dewdrops.

"Where did Dad say the bus stop is again?" I asked.

Jeff pointed. "At the bottom of the hill, along that road there." I sighed. The road looked far, far away, like a narrow gray ribbon running through the green fields.

"Race you," Jeff said. He sprinted ahead of me.

I ran after him. Jeff's a shrimp for his age, while I'm exactly average, so I passed him without any trouble.

"Wait up," Jeff called.

I ignored him. Even though I usually hate exercise, it actually felt good to run as fast as I could, breathing in the fresh morning air. *In some ways, living in the country might not be so bad,* I thought.

"Hey," a voice said in front of me. "Where are you going in such a hurry?"

I stopped short and looked up. A boy with smooth blond hair and almond-shaped, greenish eyes was standing there. For a moment I had a funny feeling I knew him from somewhere, but as I got closer I realized I'd never seen him before.

"I'm running for the school bus," I gasped.

The boy chuckled. "You must be new here," he drawled. "The bus is always late. It won't be here for another ten minutes."

"How do you know?"

The boy smiled. He had a nice smile, slow and lazy-looking. "Because I've lived around here forever," he replied, laughing. "What's your name?"

"A-Amanda," I stuttered. I was nervous because the more I looked at the boy, the more I realized how good-looking he was. Even cuter than Roger Jones, who my friends and I agreed was far and away the cutest boy at Saint Hilda's.

"And him?" The boy pointed at Jeff, who came up panting.

"He's my little brother, Jeff."

"Hi, Amanda. Hi, Jeff." The boy smiled his slow, lazy smile again. I glanced at Jeff. He was scowling.

"Who are you?" he asked rudely.

The boy put out his hand. "I'm Will."

Jeff didn't shake Will's outstretched hand. I glared at my brother. It wasn't like him to be so rude.

"Will lives around here. I guess he's a neighbor of ours," I said quickly.

"Hi, neighbor," Jeff muttered. He nudged me. "Come on, Amanda. We've got to hurry or we'll miss the bus."

"Will says the bus is always late," I retorted, but Jeff was already walking. I followed, and Will walked along

33

beside me. The road narrowed, and we passed under some ancient oak trees. I glanced over at Will. I was worried he'd be offended by Jeff's rudeness, but he was still smiling. What was more, he was definitely smiling at me.

I grinned to myself, thinking that now at least I could tell Marriane I had met a boy. Not that I cared, but—

"So, are you folks building a house here?" Will asked.

"No. We moved into the old Ryland place. My dad inherited it from his great-aunt."

"The old Ryland place," Will repeated.

Something in his voice made me lift my head. Will was staring at me intently, his eyes glowing. "Are you Rylands, then?"

"Yes—" I started to say when Jeff tugged at my arm.

"Amanda," he said, his voice high and scared-sounding. "What's that weird smell?"

I sniffed, then I froze. It smelled like something was burning close by! I glanced over at Will. "Do you smell something burning?"

"That's just wood smoke," Will explained. "Lots of people around here still heat their houses with wood stoves. It gets pretty cold at night."

"Oh. Can I ask you a question?" I said boldly. "Why did you look so surprised when I said we'd moved into the old Ryland place?"

Will looked uncomfortable. "No reason. I just heard . . . well, I heard stories."

"What kind of stories?"

"Well, folks say the old lady who lived there was crazy."

I frowned, thinking of the picture of Great-Aunt Libby in the living room. She didn't *look* crazy, but there was something about the house that didn't feel right. *I've never, ever had a nightmare as vivid as the one I had last night,* I thought with a shudder, remembering the gleam of the goblin's eyes as he held me in the flames.

"And there was the fire," Will added quietly.

"How did it start?" I asked, trying hard to keep my voice casual.

Will looked at his feet. "I don't know," he answered. "It happened a long, long time ago."

From the look on his face, I had the impression he knew more about it but didn't want to say.

"So you don't have any idea what caused it?" I pressed.

His green eyes locked onto mine. I caught my breath. He looked almost angry. "Why do you want to know?" he demanded.

"I'm just curious," I replied awkwardly.

Will's face relaxed. "I can understand that. Look, I hope I didn't insult you, Amanda. I mean, I shouldn't have called your aunt crazy."

"That's okay," I said. "I never really knew her. I met her only once when I was small."

Will grinned at me. "She was always nice to me when I was little, to tell the truth. She used to give us jars of crab apple jelly she made from the crab apples on the tree by your barn. It was some jelly." I smiled. Will had a funny way of talking, sort of old-fashioned, but that was probably just from growing up in the country.

"Anyway, there aren't many kids our age out here," Will continued, "so I hope we can be friends. I could show you around the place. I know every inch of this part of the valley."

"That would be wonderful—" I started to answer when Jeff shouted, "Amanda, hurry, it's the bus!"

I quickly turned around. The bright yellow school bus was tooling down the road toward us. As it reached the corner, it pulled over. The driver, a middle-aged woman with cheeks like ripe apples, waved. "Hey, you must be the new kids," she called as the doors opened. "Amanda and Jeff Ryland, right?"

"Right," I said.

"I'm Mrs. Perkins, your bus driver."

"Hi." I smiled and turned to look for Will. I was expecting him to get on the bus with us. I was hoping he'd even want to sit with us—or at least with me.

But Will was nowhere in sight.

Chapter 6

Jeff and I flopped down in the nearest open seats. I craned my neck to look out the window, but there was still no sign of Will. "How could he have vanished like that?" I murmured.

"I'm glad he took off," Jeff said in a low voice.

I stared at my brother. "Why?"

"I don't know. I just didn't like him," Jeff said stubbornly.

"You're weird." I peered out the window again.

"What's the matter?" said a voice behind me. "Did you lose something?"

I turned my head. A girl in the seat behind us was eyeing me curiously. She was skinny, with long brown hair and a splash of light brown freckles across her nose. But she didn't look one bit like a country girl. She had on a shiny red minidress and a big rhinestone and pearl necklace with earrings to match. Around her neck, she had what looked like an old feather boa! She was dressed even wackier than Marriane, who was the wackiest dresser I knew.

"So what did you lose?" the girl repeated.

"Nothing," I replied. "It's just . . . this boy walked us to the bus stop. I thought he was going to ride the bus with us, and suddenly he disappeared." *Just like a ghost,* I added to myself with a shiver.

The girl's calm brown eyes met mine, and for some reason I felt embarrassed—as if she knew what I'd been thinking. "Oh, it was probably just Will Fowler," she said with a shrug.

"Will Fowler," I repeated. I remembered the day we first drove up to look at the farm, we'd passed an old, beat-up-looking shack. "That's the Fowlers' house," my dad had said. "They're our closest neighbors. I believe they have kids your age."

"He lives up by you all," the girl was saying. "But he's in ninth grade, so he takes the bus to the high school in Fulton."

"You mean Haneytown doesn't have a high school?" I burst out.

"Nope." The girl shook her head. "But Fulton's the next town over. Just forty miles down the road."

"Forty miles?" I repeated. "Wow! The whole island of Manhattan is only eleven miles long!"

"Eleven and a half," the girl corrected me. Her brown eyes shone. "You must be the people from New York who moved into the old Ryland place! I'm Laura Cartwright. I've just been dying to meet you!"

"What for?" demanded Jeff. I glared at him. I couldn't understand what had gotten into my brother this morning. He was being impossible!

"Because I've always wanted to visit New York," Laura replied calmly. "I was hoping you could tell me all about it. I've read all the books I can find about the city, but it isn't the same."

"It sure isn't," I agreed. "It's nice to meet you. I'm Amanda Ryland and this is my brother, Jeff."

"Hi. Welcome to Haneytown. I keep trying to get Chris—that's my dad—to take me to New York City, but he thinks it's just this big, dangerous place. He runs the town paper," she explained in a rush.

"Oh," I said. I was starting to like this girl. Her clothes might be weird, but at least she had the good taste to like the city, even if she'd never been there. I thought it was cool that she called her dad by his first name. I read somewhere that movie stars' kids did that all the time. "So why are you so interested in New York?"

"I want to be an actress when I grow up," Laura declared, her eyes shining. "And that's where all actresses go—Broadway, New York. If they don't go to Hollywood, that is."

"Mmmm," I said, suppressing a grin. No wonder she reminded me of Marriane!

The bus was winding through green rolling hills now, stopping every so often to pick up more kids. Even so, it was still half empty. I found myself wondering how many kids were in this school.

"There are only fifty of us," Laura said.

I gazed at her in surprise. "I can read minds sometimes if it's someone I like," Laura explained in answer to a question I hadn't asked. "My grandmother May was a spiritualist, and—"

"A what?" Jeff broke in.

"She talked to ghosts," Laura replied.

"Ghosts?" I stared at her. "You're kidding, right?"

But Laura shook her head. "No. Grandma May really did." A look of pain came into her deep brown eyes. "Until she passed away two years ago, she was always being consulted by people around here. She hoped I'd take over for her one day, but I don't have her gift of communicating with spirits. My mom had it, but she died when I was born."

"Oh," I said awkwardly.

"It's all right. I never knew her," Laura said softly. "I really miss my Grandma May, though. Your Great-Aunt Libby used to come see her sometimes."

I suddenly felt cold. "What about?" I asked.

Laura looked uneasy. "I think she believed your house was haunted," she whispered.

I thought of what Tara or Marriane would say if they could hear this conversation. Tara would roll her eyes and shriek, "Amanda, give me a break!" "Yeah, really," Marriane would put in. "Only total nut cases believe in ghosts." As recently as yesterday morning I would have agreed with them, but now I wasn't so sure.

"It had something to do with the fire, didn't it?" Jeff said. I glanced at my brother in surprise. He didn't sound like he was asking a question. He sounded like he knew.

Laura looked at both of us, then nodded. "I think so."

"I wish I knew more about the fire," I said. "My dad won't talk about it. Neither will my mom. They just keep saying it happened a long time ago and we should forget about it."

The bus turned off the road and started up a long dirt driveway. Around us, kids were talking and laughing, and Mrs. Perkins cleared her throat and called out, "Children, behave yourselves!"

Laura suddenly leaned toward me. "I'll bet I could find out about it for you," she told me softly. "My dad has files of old newspapers from Haneytown going back a hundred years. There must be articles about the fire. I could make copies for you."

"Could you? That'd be great!"

"Sure. I'll go through the files this afternoon." Laura smiled at me. "Then I could call you tonight and let you know. It's too bad you're not on the Net, because then—"

"The Net?" I exclaimed. "You're on-line?"

Laura laughed. "Of course I am. It's hard to live in a little place like this without being on-line. I talk to people from all over. I even have a couple of pals from New York," she added proudly.

"So do I," I said with a sigh. Then I had an idea. "Listen, my friends and I have our own chat room. I could give you the address, and maybe you could meet my friends, too." I dug into my backpack and pulled out a new notebook and pen. I flipped to the first page and wrote out our chat room address. It wasn't like me to be so friendly so quickly, but even though we'd just met, I'd already decided I liked Laura a lot. "One of my friends, Marriane, wants to be an actress, just like you. The other one wants to be a fashion designer."

"Are you serious?" Laura flashed me a wide grin as I tore the page out of my notebook and handed it to her. "That would be *sooo* fabulous!" Then she glanced at me. "What about you?"

"What about me?" I asked.

"What do you want to be? You told me what your friends want to do. What about you?"

I shrugged. "I don't know yet," I admitted. "My friends are both talented. They both have things they're really good at. But I'm just ordinary."

"No one is just ordinary," said Laura.

"I am," I replied, smiling.

Just then Mrs. Perkins pulled the bus to a shuddering halt. I looked up, and my heart sank. This couldn't be my new school. "It's so small!" I gasped. "It looks like a garage."

"It's not that small," Laura retorted. "There are six classrooms—and the office, of course. I'll take you in and introduce you to our teacher, Mrs. Butternut."

"Mrs. Butternut?" I repeated. I could imagine what this woman would look like: eighty years old with gray hair and funny glasses with rhinestones. I couldn't believe my parents would put me in a place like this.

Laura giggled. "I have a feeling you're going to get a real surprise when you see Mrs. Butternut. Come on."

"Let's go, Jeff," I said. But to my surprise, Jeff had already gotten off the bus. I could see his red hair streaking across the parking lot.

"That's funny," I murmured. My little brother was usually pretty shy about going into new places, but he was moving as if he knew exactly where he was going. *Or maybe he's just mad because I'm making new friends already and he isn't.* I remembered how rude he'd been all morning.

Absorbed in my thoughts, I followed Laura off the bus.

Chapter 7

Mrs. Butternut pointed at the map. "This is Tanzania, an east African country that won independence from Great Britain in—" Before our teacher could finish, a bell rang so loudly that the windows rattled.

"Oops!" Mrs. Butternut turned to the class. "Lunchtime! Okay, everyone is excused. We'll continue our discussion this afternoon. And don't knock each other over!" she called out as a bunch of kids dashed toward the door.

She smiled down at me. "Did you bring lunch, Amanda?" she asked kindly. "I'm afraid we don't have a cafeteria here."

"It's okay. My mom packed me a bagel and cream cheese."

Mrs. Butternut's smile got wider. "A bagel!" She sighed dreamily. "If there's one thing I miss about New York, it's good bagels."

I smiled back. Laura was right about Mrs. Butternut being a big surprise. For one thing, she was only about twenty-eight. For another, she was definitely stylish, with short, spiky blond hair and really cool clothes. And she was from the city, just like me!

"See you this afternoon, Amanda." Mrs. Butternut

waved, and I headed for the door. I was feeling a little shy all of a sudden, but then I saw Laura waiting for me.

"Come on," she said warmly as we walked outside. "I'm going to take you to my favorite lunch spot." I followed her across the crowded playing field. At the end of the field was an old elm tree. Laura sat down cross-legged among the large twisted roots. "Look," she said, pointing. "You can see the whole valley from here."

The elm tree was on a little hill, and from there you could see farmhouses and green fields and, beyond, the greeny-blue peaks of the White Mountains. I'd have to ask Laura why they were called the White Mountains. I blinked as a bright flash of blue passed by overhead. "What was that?"

"A mountain bluebird," Laura explained. "They're just coming back now."

"Coming back from where?"

"Down south, of course," Laura said. "They migrate every fall. Then they come back when it's spring again."

"Oh," I said. I'd never paid attention to any birds except the pigeons that lived on the windowsills outside our apartment. It was funny. I'd been so sure I wouldn't learn anything new living in the country, but maybe I was wrong. I took a bite of my bagel. A blond boy ran past us. The color of his hair made me think of Will.

"So what's Will Fowler like?" I asked, trying to sound casual.

Laura shrugged. "I don't really know him. His family just moved back last year." She suddenly laughed. "I hear he's really cute, though. Sally Mason—that red-haired girl in our class—has a major crush on him."

44

"Oh. Well, he is sort of cute, I guess, if that's your type," I said. Laura grinned, and I felt my face turn hot.

"So did your grandmother really talk to ghosts?" I asked, quickly changing the subject. "Or were you just making that up?"

Laura shook her head. "She really did. People came from all over the valley to talk to their relatives who'd passed on."

"What about?"

Oh, regular stuff mostly. Like when they should pick their apples or where to plant certain crops."

I giggled. "People ask ghosts where to plant crops?"

Laura giggled, too. "I know it sounds crazy, but it isn't, really. Say you're a farmer, and your granddad farmed the same land for sixty years before you. His spirit would probably know more about where to plant corn than you would."

"Yeah, but I thought people would ask about more exciting stuff. Like who they were going to marry or if they would become rich and famous or win the lottery."

Laura frowned. "People aren't like that around here," she said seriously. "Most folks are pretty happy with life as it comes. They just want advice about everyday things." She giggled again. "Grandma used to go crazy because every year all these old ladies would come to get recipes from their relatives who'd died."

"Recipes?"

"Sure, for pie or apple butter." Laura rolled her eyes. "Grandma used to say, 'Laura, can you imagine how hard it is trying to take down a recipe from a ghost?'"

I gaped at my new friend. Laura sounded so calm, so matter-of-fact, you'd never dream she was talking about *ghosts*.

"Bizarre," I said. "Laura, do you really believe in that stuff?"

She hesitated. "Yeah, I guess I do," she replied slowly. "You know how some houses feel good and some feel kind of strange and spooky?"

I shivered, thinking of the feeling I had in *our* new house. "I guess so."

"Well, when people leave this world, they leave traces of themselves behind." Laura's voice became distant. "Sometimes the traces are strong and sometimes they're not, depending on what happened to the people in this world. It's like pieces of them are still floating around. Most ghosts are happy, but some aren't. The ones that are still searching for rest are the ones you have to worry about, Grandma May always said."

"What about goblins?" I said softly.

"Goblins?" Laura eyed me curiously. "Like what?"

I blushed, feeling embarrassed. What was I doing talking about my weird dream to this girl I hardly knew? "Oh, nothing," I said quickly. "I just had a funny dream last night. I saw a monster that looked like a goblin or a gremlin or something. It seemed so real. I've never had a dream like that before. I know those things aren't supposed to exist, but if ghosts do . . ."

"Grandma May told me about spirits like that," Laura replied slowly. "She said that when people did something *really* bad in this world, you could tell because their spirits didn't look human anymore. They looked like horrendous monsters."

"That's creepy," I said.

Laura nodded. "I guess so, but it makes sense in a way. Grandma May used to say the best thing about talking to spirits was that it helped you see things as they really were. She said you could see what people were really made of." Laura shook herself. "Sometimes I wish I did have Grandma May's talent for speaking to the spirits," she added quietly.

"How do you know you don't?"

"Because Grandma tried to get the spirits to talk to me a million times, but they never would."

I opened my mouth to ask Laura about the ghost in our house—the one Great-Aunt Libby consulted Laura's grandmother about—but before I could get the words out, I heard yelling at the other end of the playground.

"It's burning! Get Mr. Gordon!"

Mr. Gordon was the principal. Laura had shown me his office, a tiny cubicle next to the front entrance of the school.

"He set fire to the grass!" a boy shouted, dashing past us.

Laura leaped to her feet. "Who did?" she called.

"That new kid! He's nuts!"

My heart started thudding. *Jeff?* I glanced around wildly. A clump of grass at the edge of the playing field was on fire. A bunch of kids were gathered around the flames, and they were holding on to someone. My brother!

"He did it. I saw him!" a tall blond kid shouted.

I sprang up and ran. By the time I got to the end of the field, a group of boys had put out the fire with a hose, but the air still smelled of ashes. I pushed through the crowd of kids. They were all shouting and talking at once. "He did it! The new kid! It was him!"

"Jeff," I sputtered. "What's going on?"

Jeff looked up at me. Tears had formed in his eyes, and he looked small and scared. "I don't know, Mandy," he whispered.

My heart turned over. Jeff hadn't called me Mandy since he was a baby, when he couldn't pronounce Amanda.

I reached out and took his hand.

There was a pack of matches in it.

"Where did you get these?" I cried.

"He's a pyromaniac," the blond boy shouted. "That's what happens to people who grow up in New York City. They go nutso. Plus he's a Ryland."

"What's that supposed to mean?" I demanded fiercely.

"Everyone knows all Rylands are crazy, especially us Fowlers," the blond boy said, tightening his grip on my brother's arm. I stared at him in shock. No wonder he looked like Will Fowler. He must be his younger brother. But why was he being so nasty to us? Why did he say all Rylands were crazy?

I yanked Jeff away from him. "You don't know what you're talking about," I faltered.

"Yeah," put in a familiar voice beside me. "The Rylands are no crazier than anyone else!" It was Laura. I glanced at her gratefully. "Now everyone move back," she ordered firmly. "Can't you see this kid's about to faint?"

I turned my eyes back to Jeff. His face was gray, and his breathing was shallow. My heart began to pound faster as I crouched down beside him. "Jeff, are you okay?" I said softly.

Jeff shuddered. "I . . . I think so."

"You've got to tell me what happened."

"I don't know," Jeff moaned.

"Well, tell me what you do know."

"Yes, tell us what you did!" boomed a voice.

It was our principal, Mr. Gordon, and he looked mad.

"Luckily those boys thought quickly and put that fire out," Mr. Gordon said grimly, "because around here a grass fire can easily burn out of control. No one, I repeat, *no one,* is allowed to use matches in this school. What made you do it, son? What were you thinking?"

"I—" Jeff slumped backward. Then he whispered something so softly, I think I was the only one who heard him. "It wasn't me. It was Billy."

"Who's Billy?" I asked.

But Jeff just put his hands over his face.

I lifted my head. "Is there anyone named Billy here?"

"No. Why?" said the blond boy rudely.

"Because my brother says someone called Billy set the fire, not him!"

"He's lying," the blond boy retorted. "He was all alone out here. Ask anyone. He's just crazy."

"That's enough out of you, Jed Fowler," Mr. Gordon said sternly. The blond boy took a step backward, then spun around and walked away.

I turned back to Jeff. "What did Billy look like?" I hissed, but Jeff didn't respond. He rose shakily to his feet.

"I think we'd better go to my office," said Mr. Gordon. He put his hand on Jeff's shoulder and started leading him across the field. I stood up and followed after them. Mr. Gordon hadn't asked me to come, but I couldn't leave my brother to face this alone. As I wove through the crowd of kids, Laura stepped forward. "Amanda, I'll tell Mrs. Butternut where you are, and I'll talk to you later," she said, squeezing my shoulder.

I nodded, heartsick. For my brother and me, the first day at our new school had turned out to be the biggest disaster of our lives. And the worst part was, I couldn't understand how it had happened. Jeff could be mischievous and obnoxious sometimes, just like any little kid, but he had never done anything like this before. Mr. Gordon looked angry, but he had reason to be.

Setting fires was serious trouble!

Chapter 8

"**I**'ve put Jeff to bed," Mom announced as she came into the dining room and sat down. "As soon as his head hit the pillow, he fell fast asleep." The three of us had finished supper, but no one felt up to clearing the table, washing the dishes, or doing anything normal like that.

"I wonder if we should take him to the doctor, Dan," my mom said in a low voice. "He isn't acting like himself."

My father hunched his shoulders. "Maybe we should," he murmured. He looked up at me. "Amanda, did you see Jeff set that fire at school?"

I gulped. "Not exactly. But when I went over there, he was holding matches in his hand," I said miserably.

After talking to my parents, Mr. Gordon had agreed not to expel Jeff, but he had suspended him for three days. He'd also told my parents they needed to have a serious talk with my brother. "Maybe he's resentful about the move," Mr. Gordon had suggested as the three of us left his office.

"And you don't think one of the other kids set the fire?" Dad asked.

I shook my head. "But Jeff did say . . ." My voice trailed off. What could I tell my parents? *Jeff said some* kid called Billy did it—only Billy doesn't exist? I stared down at my feet.

"What does Jeff say?" my mother prompted.

"You know what Jeff says!" my dad exclaimed. "He says he didn't do it. He keeps saying that over and over."

"No, he doesn't, dear," Mom corrected him gently. "He says he doesn't remember."

"Either way, it isn't like Jeff to refuse to take responsibility for his actions," said Dad.

A door slammed somewhere upstairs. *Maybe it's the ghost again,* I thought, and I shivered. Making jokes about ghosts didn't seem one bit funny anymore.

"No, it isn't," Mom agreed tiredly. "But maybe it's the move." She looked hesitantly at my father. "Dan, you and I were so eager to get out of the city we didn't even think about how hard it would be on the kids. I don't think Jeff and Amanda want to be here. Maybe"—my mom swallowed—"maybe this is Jeff's way of showing how upset he is!" Mom turned to me, her eyes wide and dark. "I'm sorry, Amanda. I guess your dad and I were pretty thoughtless."

The day before I would have been overjoyed to hear my mom talking like this. I might have even tried to persuade her it wasn't too late to turn around and move back to the city. But now, listening to her just made me feel awful.

"It's not that bad being here," I said quickly. "Anyway, I don't think that's what's wrong with Jeff."

Mom's eyes widened. "Then what is?" she asked.

I didn't know how to answer. Instead, I started clearing the dishes without even being asked. After I was done, I excused myself, went upstairs to my room, and flopped down on my bed. I wanted to do some hard thinking, but my brain was all in a whirl. *What was happening to Jeff? Did his setting that fire have something to do with the fire here? Did ghosts exist? Could the creature I'd seen in my dream really be a spirit? If so, what did it want?*

I sat up and glanced over at my computer. Dad had finished hooking it up. Suddenly I knew what I wanted to do. I wanted to talk to my friends.

I flicked on the machine and logged myself onto the Net. Then I punched in the address for the *Superstars* chat room.

I was hoping Tara and Marriane would be there, but though I wrote *Hello, hello, call me!* over and over, there was no answer. It was about time for the spring concert at Saint Hilda's, and Tara and Marriane were both in the choir. So was I, although I wasn't a very good singer. *They're probably at choir rehearsal,* I thought hopelessly, *which is where I would be if I wasn't stuck in a haunted house.*

I was about to give up and log off when a message appeared on the screen. *Amanda, are you home?* The message was from *Lorelei.*

My heart jumped. *Who are you?* I typed.

It's me, Laura, came the answer.

I breathed a sigh of relief. *Laura!* I wrote. *Hi, what's up? I know you were hoping to meet my friends, but they're not here, unfortunately.*

That's okay. How's Jeff?

He's asleep. I guess he's all right. I don't know.

I found something. I'll show you on the school bus tomorrow.

What is it?

An article about the fire. I don't know if it'll help, but—you'd better look at it yourself.

What does it say?

I'll show it to you tomorrow. I'll save a seat for you on the bus, and Jeff, too.

Okay, I wrote back. *But it'll be just me on the bus. Jeff's staying home. Mr. Gordon suspended him for three days.*

No!

It's okay. My mom's taking him to the doctor, anyway. She's worried there's something wrong with him. I paused. *So am I,* I added.

Did he admit he started the fire?

That's what's so strange, I typed back. *He keeps saying he didn't do it. He keeps insisting he doesn't remember any of it.*

Laura didn't answer for a moment. Then she typed in, *Does he often tell lies?*

No, never, I typed back. *Well, almost never.* It was true. I know some little kids tell lies all the time, but Jeff had always been honest. If he broke something in our apartment, he always told our parents himself.

Then maybe he isn't lying, Laura wrote.

I gulped. In a way, Laura's writing that made me feel a lot better. She was telling me she believed my brother wasn't a crazy pyromaniac. But in another way it scared me. If Jeff wasn't lying, what was going on?

I have to go, Laura wrote. *Chris is yelling at me to feed Sebastian.*

Sebastian?

Our golden lab. He's sixteen years old. That's a hundred and twelve in people years, so he's pretty fussy about food—like a lot of old people I know.

Oh, I wrote.

Try not to worry, Amanda. I'll see you tomorrow, okay? Bye!

The computer buzzed, and a sign-off message appeared in the lower left-hand corner of the screen. I was all alone in the *Superstars* chat room. I stared at the keyboard. I was thinking about typing an e-mail message for Tara and Marriane. *Get in touch right away!* They would probably be worried, though. They'd think something really bad had happened. But then again, that was true.

I jumped as my computer made a soft buzzing noise. Then I froze. There was a message on the screen.

Burn, burn, burn. You will burn.

Beware. Beware. Beware Tom, Rachel.

Beware Billy!

Panic filled my body. Who could be writing this? What did it mean? I glanced at the return address. *G$$$ftaweee881.* Gibberish! I stretched out my fingers toward the keyboard. I needed to say something, but what? *Who are you and what are you talking about?* I typed.

Behind me I heard my bedroom door creak open and footsteps pad toward me. I whirled around. It was Jeff in his Superman pajamas. He had a funny, blank look in his eyes. He looked like he was still asleep.

"Jeff!" I cried.

But he didn't hear me. He moved over to the screen and stared at it. Then he started screaming.

Chapter 9

"It's him!" Jeff babbled. "It's him!"

There was such terror in his voice that I immediately thought of the goblin from my dream. I grabbed my brother by the shoulders. "Who?"

"*Him!*" Jeff screamed.

The door of my room flew open, and my mom and dad came racing in. "What's going on?" they shouted.

"It's Jeff," I replied. "He came into my room. I think he's sleepwalking. He saw my computer, and—"

I glanced at the computer, but the message was gone. In its place a single name blinked at me. "*Rachel*," I read wonderingly.

I turned back to my brother. My mom crouched down in front of him. "Jeff, what's wrong? Are you all right?"

Jeff rubbed his eyes and nodded sleepily. "I guess so. I must have been dreaming."

"What was the dream?" I burst out.

Jeff shook his head. "I don't remember," he said crossly. "Can I please go back to bed now?"

My mom and dad exchanged a glance. "Sure, Monkey," my dad said. "Come on, let's go." He took Jeff's hand, just like he used to when Jeff was little. I expected Jeff to pull away and snarl "Cut it out, Dad," the way he usually did when my parents tried to take his hand or give him a hug. Instead, Jeff just went along with him.

I swallowed. I felt as if there were a stone in my chest.

I looked up at my mom. She looked as if she were about to burst into tears. "Your father and I are taking Jeff to the doctor tomorrow morning," she whispered. Her face crumbled. "Oh, Amanda, I'm beginning to wish we never had moved here."

Me, too, I thought, but I didn't say so. I didn't want to make things any worse than they already were. I stared at the computer. The screen was totally blank again.

"Better get to bed, Amanda. You have school tomorrow," Mom said wearily as she left the room.

I flicked off my computer. Pulling on my nightgown, I crawled into bed, but I didn't go to sleep. I stared out the window and thought about the message. Who was Tom? Who was Billy? And who was Rachel? Could she be the girl in the picture? If so, she was a ghost! "And ghosts don't exist," I mumbled aloud. But if they didn't exist, who was getting into the *Superstars* chat room?

I had a feeling Laura's old newspaper article might give me some answers, but would it help me figure out what was happening to my brother? The moon rose over the mountains, casting a ghostly light on the pasture. I thought I saw someone—a blond head moving across the field. *Will Fowler,* I thought, *or his brother, Jed.* A chill stole over me as I remembered how Jed had acted on the playground. Why had he been so sure Jeff had set the fire? Why had he said all the Rylands were crazy? My heart in my mouth, I sat up, pressed my face to the glass, and stared.

The field was empty.

Chapter 10

I peered down the road, looking for the school bus. It was already ten past eight and the bus was nowhere in sight. A thick fog had settled over the valley overnight. I looked up, scrunching my eyes. The fog was so dense you couldn't even see the mountains. A twig snapped behind me. I spun around.

It was Will Fowler.

"Hi," he said, giving me a friendly wave. "I was hoping I'd see you this morning. Where's your brother?"

"He's staying home today," I replied. "Didn't your brother, Jed, tell you?"

Will looked bewildered for a moment. "Jed? He's not my brother. He's my cousin. I haven't seen him for a while." He eyed me curiously. "Did he give you a hard time?"

I shrugged. "Not exactly." I knew I should tell Will what had happened at school yesterday, but I couldn't bring myself to do it. I kept thinking about what his cousin had said: *All Rylands are crazy!* Probably that was what everyone at school thought now, but I didn't want Will to think it, too.

I stared at my feet a moment. "Anyway, it sure is foggy this morning," I said awkwardly. "It makes me feel kind of claustrophobic."

Will smiled his lazy grin. He was even better-looking than I remembered. I blushed as I thought of what Marriane would say if she saw him: *A total fox!*

"That's just because you're not used to it," he said. "When you've lived here awhile, you'll get to like the fog."

"Have you always lived here?" I asked.

"Yep. I've never been anywhere else. And if I have my way, I'll stay here forever," Will answered. His green eyes flashed. "This corner of the valley is my place, my home," he added softly. "I belong here."

"Oh," I said. I stared at him curiously. Something about what he said bothered me, but I didn't know what. I loved New York, but it sounded like he loved this valley even more than I loved the city.

"You have to know the valley to understand how I feel about it," Will went on. "How about this weekend I take you for a hike up in the hills? I'll show you where the old peach orchards are, and where wild raspberries grow. Your brother can come along, too . . . if he wants," he added, a little reluctantly.

My cheeks suddenly felt warm. It was almost like being asked on a date. Of course it wasn't a date, but still . . . "Sure, I'd like that," I said shyly, but then my stomach turned over. I wondered if Will would drop the invitation when he heard about what Jeff had done.

I opened my mouth to tell him it might not be such a good idea, but before I could get the words out, Will flashed me a grin. "Great. I've got to go now!"

He turned and disappeared into the fog. I stared after him until I heard the honking of the school bus.

Laura was sitting way in the back.

"I saved you a seat," she whispered. "How's your brother?"

I sighed. "Not too good," I said. "It—"

I noticed the kids in the row ahead were listening. In fact, they were all staring at me with funny looks on their faces.

All Rylands are crazy! I could almost hear Jed Fowler's voice in my head.

"I'll tell you later," I said hurriedly.

Laura nodded. "Good idea." She pulled a manila envelope out of her backpack. "Here, take a look at this."

Inside the envelope were a couple of stapled pages. I stared at the top one. It was a copy of the front page of the *Haneytown Herald.* "Fire Tragedy at Ryland Farm," blared the headline. I looked at the date of the paper: June 7, 1932.

June 7, 1932? I thought. *Why does that date sound so familiar?* Then I remembered. It was the date the clock on my computer had switched to the day Dad hooked us up—the day we talked to the strangers who said they were ghosts!

My mouth went dry. I looked at Laura.

"Go on, read the rest," she said.

I nodded dumbly. As the bus made its slow, sleepy way through the fog, I pulled the article closer and started to read.

Police are almost certain the fire was started by Tom Ryland, age nine. The young Ryland boy had recently gotten in trouble for setting several fires. Dr. Alexander Grayfield, professor of psychiatry at Hampshire Hills Hospital in Concord, said such pyromania is unusual but by no means unheard of in such a young child. "Perhaps if Tom had received help earlier, this tragedy could have been avoided," Dr. Grayfield declared. The fatalities included Arthur and Molly Ryland, Rachel Ryland, age twelve, and Tom Ryland.

I caught my breath. So Tom and Rachel were the children who had died in the fire! I thought of the photograph of Tom and Rachel that Jeff and I had found in the attic. They had looked like a normal sister and brother. You'd never guess in a million years that the little boy would set a fire that would kill his whole family.

I shuddered and read on. *Also believed to have perished in the fire is neighbor Billy Fowler, age thirteen, a friend of Tom and Rachel's. Investigators are still searching for his body.*

I rested the paper on my knees, feeling sick and dizzy. Now I understood why my parents hadn't wanted to talk about the fire. I also understood why Will Fowler had acted so strangely when I brought it up, and why Jed Fowler had insisted that all the Rylands were crazy. I had hoped Laura's newspaper article would give me some answers, and it had. I closed my eyes, remembering the message on my computer the night before. *Beware Tom, Rachel. Beware Billy!*

I remembered Laura telling me that if anyone had done something really bad in this world, their spirit didn't look human anymore. Could the goblin I'd seen in my dream be the ghost of Tom Ryland? I clapped my hand over my mouth. The answer was right in front of me, but I didn't want to believe it. Tom Ryland had been a pyromaniac. He'd set a fire that killed all those people. And now my brother was setting fires and acting weird. There was only one explanation I could think of, even though it sounded crazy. Rachel's ghost was warning me to beware of Tom, because Tom was coming back.

And he was taking over my little brother!

Chapter 11

"There's only one thing we can do," Laura said. "We have to hold a seance."

It was after school, and we were sitting on Laura's front porch drinking iced tea.

"A what?" I asked dully. My day hadn't gone all that well. Everyone at school was talking about how Jeff had set the playground on fire. Everywhere I went, kids stared at me or whispered behind my back. It was bad enough being the new kid in school, but now that everyone had decided my brother and I were crazy, it was a zillion times worse. If Laura hadn't invited me to her house after school, I probably would have gone home and cried my eyes out. Instead, I had just finished telling Laura about all the weird things that had happened since we'd moved into the old Ryland house.

"A seance," Laura repeated.

I stared at her. "Very funny."

"I'm not joking," Laura said firmly. "We have to talk to the ghosts. We have to find out what Rachel knows."

Even though the fog had burned off and the day had turned warm and sunny, I suddenly felt cold all over. "What if the ghosts don't want to talk?" I said miserably. "Anyway, maybe there aren't any ghosts. How do I know there are ghosts? Because I had a bad dream? Because my brother's acting strange? Because someone on the Net wrote they were from Ghostweb? That even sounds like a joke!"

Laura shook her head. "No, it doesn't," she said. "The fact that they said they were from Ghostweb is one reason I'm sure there really are ghosts trying to contact you."

"Huh?"

"That's what Grandma May always called the spirit world," Laura continued, her eyes shining. "The web. She called it the web because she said the spirits think of themselves as a web of energy spreading over the world. It's out there, but you have to be able to access it. Most ghosts can't act or speak on their own. They need the energy of living people to help them."

She frowned. "Wicked ghosts, or the spirits of people who did bad things in this world, are usually trapped here. They can't find rest. They're the ghosts you hear about most of the time—the ones that slam windows and doors, put out lights. But most spirits are happy where they are. That's why they need to be called before they'll come back here. They need minds willing to call them back to earth, to let them cross over from the spirit world. That's why mediums are so important. That's what Grandma May always said."

"But I'm not trying to get in touch with them!" I reminded her. "They're trying to get in touch with me."

"That must mean they have something important to tell you," Laura explained.

"Or maybe I'm just crazy," I said glumly. "Or Jeff is."

Laura's brown eyes bored into my blue ones. "I don't think so," she replied. "From what I've seen, you don't seem one bit like a crazy person. And neither does Jeff," she added. "Until he set that fire, I would have sworn he was a regular little kid."

I let out a deep, shuddering breath. "Me, too," I murmured. "That's what makes this whole thing so strange."

"And dangerous," Laura chimed in. Her normally cheerful face looked anxious. "If only Grandma May were still alive, she'd know what to do for sure." Laura sighed. "I know she was worried about your Great-Aunt Libby. She told me so one of the last times your aunt came to see her."

"Did your grandmother say why she was worried?" I broke in.

"No, not exactly. All Grandma said was . . . let me see if I can remember." Laura screwed up her eyes in concentration. "She said there was something about the situation she didn't understand."

"That's all?"

Laura nodded. "She wouldn't tell me more. I wasn't that interested, either, to tell you the truth," she went on quietly. "Grandma was already sick by then, and I was worried about that. Plus, I didn't want to hear about any spirit stuff, because"—Laura drew in a breath and let it out—"I guess I was scared Grandma was disappointed in me for not being able to talk to the spirits," she finished awkwardly.

"I bet she was never disappointed in you," I said.

Laura smiled sadly. "Whatever. Anyway, now I wish I'd listened harder to Grandma May's stories, because I'd have a better idea what to do. Still, a seance is a good start."

Something about the determined way Laura said this

made me feel all shaky inside. I could hardly believe the two of us were seriously talking about holding a seance. *Still, what choice do we have?* I thought. A knot formed in my stomach as I remembered the horrible creature in my dream, and Jeff's pale face and blank eyes the day the playground had caught fire. I glanced at Laura. I was lucky to have her for a friend. If it weren't for her, Jeff and I would be facing this all alone.

"So where should we hold the seance? At your house?"

Laura shook her head. "It'll have to be at your house," she replied simply. "Grandma May always said in cases of possession, you have to go to the source."

"The source?" I repeated.

"The place where you feel the ghost's presence most strongly," Laura replied gravely. "Ghosts tend to come back to places they know."

For some reason, when Laura said that, it made me think of Will Fowler's words that morning. *I belong here.* And I remembered the day we moved into our house. My dad had said, "It feels great to be back here. You know, Amanda, Jeff, there have been Rylands in this valley for hundreds of years." I peered down the hill in front of Laura's house at the farmhouses and fields and orchards of Haneytown.

I'm a Ryland, I thought. *So I guess I belong here, too.* But the idea didn't make me happy. Instead, I felt even more afraid. Maybe I belonged here, but that wasn't necessarily a good thing, especially if it meant that the ghost of Rachel Ryland was haunting me and the ghost of Tom Ryland was taking over my brother.

"So I think Friday I should spend the night and—"

"Are you sure that'll be okay with your dad?" I asked.

Laura laughed. "Chris? He wouldn't mind one bit. He knows I can take care of myself. Besides, he's so absentminded it would probably take him a couple of days to even notice I was gone."

I laughed, too. Then I eyed Laura thoughtfully. Despite living in such a small place all her life, in some ways she was more grown-up than I was. And despite her wacky clothes and all her talk about ghosts, she was a solid person underneath. It proved that my mom was right: You couldn't judge people by where they were from or how they looked.

I smiled at her. "I'm lucky you're my friend."

Laura rolled her eyes. "I'm the one who's lucky," she said stoutly. "Thanks to you, when I do make it to the city, I won't be totally clueless!" Her face became serious again. "So remember to get permission from your parents to have me spend the night on Friday and we'll take it from there."

I nodded. I was sure my mom would say yes. The day after tomorrow Laura and I were going to hold a real, honest-to-goodness seance. We were going to talk to the ghosts of Rachel and Tom. For a second, I longed to tell Laura to forget about the seance, but I knew I couldn't.

Whatever was happening to my brother and me was real—and dangerous. I could feel it in my bones. It might even be a matter of life and death!

Chapter 12

Mom puffed out her cheeks. "I don't know what to do," she declared. "I'd really like to go to the Coopers' house with your dad, but I don't know about leaving you kids alone."

It was Friday, and Laura's dad had just dropped her off. Mom had given the okay for Laura spend the night, but at the last minute, Dr. and Mrs. Cooper, our closest neighbors except for the Fowlers, had invited Mom and Dad to dinner. Dad really wanted to go because Dr. Cooper knew all the great fishing spots in the neighborhood, and Mom wanted Mrs. Cooper's expert advice on some possible recipes for her cookbook. The only problem was that Mom didn't want to leave us alone, especially when I had a friend sleeping over.

"It's cool, Mrs. Ryland," Laura said smoothly. "We can take care of ourselves."

"Yeah, Mom, we'll be fine," I said.

Mom smiled. "Oh, I know you're both sensible and responsible enough to be left on your own," she replied. "I'm still a little worried about Jeff, Amanda. The doctor said he's perfectly fine, but something's not right. He's been sleeping a lot."

I frowned. The doctor had told my mom and dad that

Jeff was completely healthy. He said my parents shouldn't make too big a deal about the fire. "All kids act out from time to time," he had told them, "and if you make too much of this incident, you'll reinforce the negative behavior." His advice made sense, but he didn't know Jeff, so he didn't know how out of character it was for him to set a field on fire.

Out of character for Jeff, but not for Tom Ryland, I thought as a finger of fear slowly inched up my spine. "I think he's okay, Mom," I piped up, trying to sound more confident than I felt. "We'll let him watch movies until it's time for bed."

Mom thought for a moment, then gave me a grateful look. "All right, Amanda, you've talked me into it. Your dad and I will accept the Coopers' invitation. I'll let your dad know. We won't be gone that long, I promise."

"Fine," I said. My palms felt sweaty. In a way, I was glad Mom and Dad wouldn't be around when Laura and I held our seance, but in another way, I was terrified.

"I'll leave the Coopers' number by the phone, okay? And there's a pizza in the freezer for your dinner," Mom went on. "Jeff may not want to go to bed because of all the sleep he's gotten lately, but try to at least get him in his pajamas by eight-thirty, okay?" she said, gesturing at the living room, where my brother was holed up on the couch watching *Star Trek*.

"No problem, Mrs. Ryland," Laura said.

I peeked at my friend. Her face looked perfectly composed, but somehow I could sense that she was as nervous as I was.

"Oh, by the way," Mom added, "Tara called this afternoon just before you got home, Amanda. She wanted me to tell you she got your message, but she and Marriane have been having trouble getting through to the chat room."

"What kind of trouble?" I asked, my pulse quickening.

"She said she'd been running into interference, whatever that means," Mom declared. "Anyway, she'll definitely be on-line tomorrow afternoon and she wants you to get in touch for sure. She said she and Marriane really miss you."

"I miss them, too," I said.

"I wonder what kind of interference," Laura murmured.

While my mom and dad were upstairs getting dressed, Laura and I pulled the pizza out of the freezer. It was my favorite kind, pesto and ricotta. Mom had bought it at the gourmet takeout in New York and had packed it, along with lots of our favorite foods, in a cooler for the move. Laura stared at the pizza in shock.

"What's that green stuff all over it?" she asked faintly.

I grinned. "Pesto, a New York specialty. Trust me. You'll love it."

We shoved the pizza into the hot oven and waited for it to cook. We had a ton of things to discuss, but we didn't dare until my parents were safely out of the house. It took my parents forever to get ready. By the time they finally headed out the door, I was about to jump out of my skin.

"Have a good night, kids!" Dad called.

"We will," I said. I watched from the door as the station wagon pulled down the driveway. Then I closed the door and turned to Laura. "Pizza first, seance afterward," I whispered.

Jeff's movie was over, so he came and sat with us in the kitchen. For a small person, my brother can eat an incredible amount. He put away about half the pizza himself while he told us lots of dumb monster jokes. I started to relax. Jeff was acting like his normal dorky self.

"Can I watch *Godzilla* after supper?" he demanded.

"Sure, no problem."

Jeff smiled. "Cool," he breathed, drumming his fingers on the table. "Have you ever seen *Godzilla*?" he asked Laura.

"No."

"It's the best! You're going to love it!"

I cleared my throat. "Actually, we're going to hang out in my room," I murmured. Laura and I had talked about having Jeff take part in the seance, but we'd both decided it wasn't a good idea.

My little brother's face fell. "Don't you want to watch the movie with me?"

"We'll be right upstairs if you need us."

Jeff pushed out his lower lip. "I thought—I mean, I . . . You guys will be really sorry if you miss *Godzilla*. It's a classic," he finished plaintively.

My chest tightened. I had a feeling I knew what my brother was trying to say: *Don't leave me alone. I'll be scared.*

"I know, Jeff! You can watch the movie in Mom and Dad's room," I said quickly. "That way we'll be just down the hall."

"Good idea," agreed Laura.

We set Jeff up in my parents' room, with lots of pillows and an extra-large dish of rocky road ice cream with chocolate sauce.

"Remember, we'll be right here if you need us," I repeated.

Jeff nodded. Now that the film was starting, he was totally absorbed. With a nervous sigh, I turned up the volume on the TV, and Laura and I went down the hall.

"Okay," I said when we were safely in my room with the door closed. "What do we need to get started?" My voice sounded shaky even to me.

Laura pursed her lips. "Are you sure you want to do this?" she asked, looking right at me. "We could just forget it, if you want."

I hesitated. Holding a seance was definitely creepy, but then I remembered the flames on the playground and my brother's terrified eyes.

"Yeah, I do, for sure," I whispered back.

"Okay, first we need a table." Laura peered around the room. "That one will work fine." She pointed to my old night table, which I've had since I was five years old. It's pink with pictures of Sleeping Beauty on it—not exactly ideal seance furniture. Still, I dragged it out to the middle of the room. It was short enough that we could sit on the floor and still reach the top.

"The next part is harder," Laura said. "I need something Tom and Rachel Ryland might have used, something that belonged to them. You said there was a bunch of old stuff in the attic, right?"

"Yeah," I replied. The thought of going up to the attic now made my blood run cold. Besides, my dad had made me promise not to go up there. Then I remembered the photograph. I reached under my bed and pulled out my overalls. Luckily, the photo was still in the front pocket. I set it on the table.

Rachel and Tom Ryland stared up at me. I was probably imagining it, but in the dim light of sunset, the grin on Tom Ryland's face that had looked so cute before suddenly looked evil! His smiling face reminded me of the creature from my dream!

Laura glanced at the picture. "Great. It's perfect. Now we both have to touch the picture, close our eyes, and concentrate."

"Concentrate on what?" I squeaked.

"What my Grandma May always said to do was to try to make your mind totally blank," Laura replied.

"I can't do that!"

"Yes, you can. Just empty your mind of everything," Laura commanded. "Think of your mind as a closet stuffed full of junk. Now just throw all the junk away."

I visualized my closet back in New York just before we moved, crammed with clothes, shoes, a basketball, and my old collection of stuffed animals. Then I visualized it as it was when we'd finished packing. Completely empty.

"Now try to see a door," said Laura. Her voice sounded distant, almost spooky. "A door into the other world."

I closed my eyes tighter. At first, all I could see was dark, empty space. Then little by little I imagined an outline of a door, surrounded by light. I thought of the dream I'd had my first night in the house—the dream where Rachel had appeared and tried to tug me into a door of flames—but quickly forced it from my thoughts.

"Okay, I see a door. What do I do now?"

"Open your mind and ask the ghosts to come in," Laura breathed.

"I don't think I can."

"Just ask them!"

"All right." My nose was prickling as if I were about to sneeze. "R-R-Rachel, if you're there, come talk to us," I stuttered.

"Yes," intoned Laura. "Come tell us what you know!"

We sat in the stillness. I could hear the numbers on my alarm clock move and the wind outside whistling across the grass. From my parents' room, I could hear people on the video shouting, "It's Godzilla!" I suddenly felt silly. *This is ridiculous! Ghosts don't exist! Of course nothing is going to happen!* I told myself. Just then the table moved.

"Laura?" I gasped.

"I hit it with my foot. Sorry," Laura muttered. "Sometimes it takes a while," she added apologetically. "Let's try again."

Once more, I closed my eyes and concentrated. "Rachel, Tom, we need to talk to you." Laura was calling the ghosts again. I opened my eyes slightly and saw that the door to my room was surrounded by orange light. The door swung open, and a girl stood there.

"Rachel!" I cried. I could actually hear the door creaking. Then I realized it wasn't the door, but the faint familiar buzzing of my computer. I opened my eyes all the way.

"The table's not moving." Laura sighed. "I don't know if this is going to work. I guess I really don't have any talent for this . . ."

I reached out and grabbed her arm.

"Laura, look!" I cried.

I pointed at my computer. Laura's eyes followed my hand, and she let out a gasp.

My computer was on, and the screen was filling up with words.

Chapter 13

Clutching each other, we crept toward my computer. The buzzing had died down, but the screen was still lit up and the words were still there.

Holding my breath, I leaned closer to read them.

Amanda, Jeff, need to talk to you . . . hard . . . trying to stop us . . . interference . . . interference!

"What does that mean?" I whispered.

Laura stirred behind me. "Grandma May told me sometimes evil ghosts try to stop other ghosts from sending messages to the living," she croaked. "Grandma called that interference. Maybe this ghost means the same thing!"

"It must be Rachel!" I exclaimed in a strangled voice. "Tom must be trying to stop her from communicating with us!"

Laura leaned over and typed a message. *Rachel, are you there?*

Yes . . . I'm . . . A bunch of random numbers and letters poured out across the screen. They looked like rows of barbed wire. This must be what Rachel meant by interference. Just then the screen went clear again, and the word *Ghostweb* appeared.

What is Ghostweb? I typed.

The computer buzzed, and a new message appeared.

All of us. But I'm Rachel. Amanda, Jeff, beware. Will happen again unless you find the truth.

The truth about what? I typed frantically.

Can't talk. Tom, Jeff, Tom, Jeff. Danger! He will not let—

My computer made a horrible screeching noise, like a car engine seizing up. I blinked, and when I looked again, the screen was blank.

"She's gone," said Laura.

I jumped as a banging noise echoed through the house.

"What was that?" I gasped.

"I don't know," Laura whispered back. "It sounded like a door slamming."

A bolt of terror shot up my spine. "Jeff!" I cried. "We'd better check on Jeff!" I dashed to the door and ran down the hall toward my parents' room. I burst through the door. The Godzilla movie was playing on the TV. People were running and screaming, as the gigantic monster came tearing down the street, ripping apart buildings with his teeth and claws. But my parents' bed was empty. Jeff was gone!

Laura came puffing up behind me. "He must have gone outside," she panted. We ran over to the window and peered out. The full moon was shining, striping the pasture with dim light. Then I saw a small figure walking slowly along the fence. It was my little brother. But where was he going? What was he doing?

The message from Rachel came pounding into my brain. *Tom, Jeff, Tom, Jeff. Danger!*

"He looks like he's sleepwalking," Laura said.

"We'd better go after him!" I shouted. "Come on, we've got to hurry!"

Chapter 14

I shivered as I slipped out the kitchen door after Laura. We hadn't even put on slippers, and the grass felt sharp and icy under my feet.

"Where is he?" Laura asked.

"Way down there. Next to the barn," I replied.

The two of us sprinted across the pasture.

The barn looked huge and dark in the pale light of the moon. I glanced around. Jeff was nowhere in sight.

What if he isn't Jeff anymore? a voice in my head screamed. *What if he's Tom Ryland now?* I thought of the photograph, of Tom Ryland's sinister grin so like that of the sneering gremlin in my dream. Then I thought of Jeff, my funny, obnoxious, know-it-all, little brother. My brother, Jeff, who wouldn't hurt a fly. My stomach lurched, and I felt like I was going to be sick.

"Where did he go?" I wailed.

"He must have gone inside the barn," Laura said worriedly.

I noticed then that the door was open a crack, wide enough for my skinny little brother to slip through, but not wide enough for Laura or me. I pulled the door, but it didn't budge.

"It's stuck," I grunted.

"I'll help you," Laura said. We both pulled as hard as we could. At last, with a loud, horrible creak, the door swung open wide.

It was dark in there, and the air smelled like hay. I could feel Laura beside me, but I was still more terrified than I'd ever been in my life. I squinted upward and saw a pair of huge yellow eyes staring down at us.

"Look!" I screamed as something moved over my head.

"It's okay. That's just a barn owl," Laura said reassuringly.

Still, we moved closer together.

"Jeff!" I called in a trembling voice. "Jeff, where are you? It's me, Mandy. Jeff?"

There was no answer, just a faint rustling over our heads.

"Jeff, where are you?" I called again.

Laura grabbed my arm. "Look up there!" I lifted my head. There was a faint, flickering light up in the hayloft. It grew brighter, and with a rising sense of horror I realized what it was: Fire!

"He must be up there!" Laura gasped. "Come on!" She pulled me through the darkness.

I dimly glimpsed a ladder in front of me. I lurched forward and started climbing it. "Jeff, Jeff, I'm coming! Hold on!" I yelled.

I could smell the fire now, a sharp prickling in my nostrils. I scrambled up to the loft. Then I stopped, paralyzed. A bale of hay in the corner was in flames. Standing over it was my brother, a strange, eager look on his face.

"Jeff!" I screamed at the top of my lungs. "What are you doing?"

Jeff's eyes met mine but seemed to look right through me. I had the most awful feeling that he didn't see me, didn't even know I was there. A sob rose in my throat. "Jeff," I cried, running over to him. "Jeff, look, it's me. Amanda!"

I stared at the bale of hay. Luckily, because of the dampness in the barn, it wasn't burning very fast, but we had to put the fire out quickly before it spread. I pulled my brother back from the sputtering flames.

I heard a scrambling sound behind me, and Laura came up the ladder huffing and puffing. In her hand, she had a metal bucket filled with water. "I found the faucet and a bucket," she said. "I hope I got enough water to douse the fire." I helped her lift the bucket up into the loft. Then I threw the water over the crackling bale of hay. The fire went out with a sizzle of smoke, and the hayloft was in total darkness again.

It took a moment or two for my eyes to adjust. When they did, I saw that Jeff was still standing near the bale of hay, staring straight ahead with a blank look on his face. I grabbed him by the arm. "What did you think you were doing?" I shouted, suddenly really mad. "You could have killed yourself!"

But Jeff just kept staring ahead blankly.

I shook him, hard. "Jeff, are you listening?"

His eyes blinked then, and a look of fear and confusion came over his face. He turned to gaze up at me. "Who are you?" he said in a high, upset voice. "What am I doing here? Where's Rachel?"

"Rachel?" I echoed.

The space around me seemed to go fuzzy for a moment, as if I were seeing it through a frosted window. Everything looked the same, but different somehow.

There was more light, for one thing—dusty golden sunlight slipping between the wooden slats in the wall. The barn looked cleaner, too—cleaner and newer. I peered down at myself and caught my breath. Instead of jeans and a T-shirt, I was wearing a long cotton nightgown trimmed with lace.

"It's okay, Tom," I heard a voice say. It was my voice and it wasn't, just like the barn was the same and wasn't. "We're going to be safe now." I reached out and took his hand. The fuzzy feeling got stronger. I felt as if I were slipping through a wall, slipping out of my own body. Then everything went dark.

Chapter 15

The next thing I knew, I was outside under the dark night sky again, still holding my brother's hand.

"Amanda?" a voice cried. "Are you okay?"

I blinked. Laura was standing in front of me. Her face looked white and scared.

"I—I think so," I stammered, panic rising in my chest as the memory of the fire in the barn came flooding back to me. "What happened?"

"Nothing." Laura lowered her voice. "You just led Jeff down the ladder, but it was like you weren't yourself!"

I drew in a breath. "I think I was—Rachel!" I whispered, horrified. "Jeff?" I shook my brother's arm. He still looked as if he were somewhere far away. Suddenly, his eyes rolled back in his head.

"Catch him!" Laura cried. "I think he going to faint!"

I reached out to grab Jeff, but I was too late. He flopped to the ground like a rag doll.

I crouched beside him. "Jeff, come on, get up!" I pleaded. He stirred, then his eyes snapped open.

"Amanda?" he said. "What's going on?" He sat up and gazed around wildly. "Where are we? What happened to *Godzilla*?"

What could I tell him? I could hardly believe what

had happened myself. There was only one explanation for it—Jeff and I had both been possessed!

"It's a long story," I said lamely. "We'd better get back in the house. Mom and Dad will be home any minute, and they'll have a fit if they find us out here."

It was a relief to worry about something as normal as getting in trouble with my parents. Jeff scrambled up, and the three of us walked shakily toward the house. We were halfway across the pasture when the funny, swimmy sensation came back again, as if the world were dissolving. I peered up ahead at the lilac bushes around the house, feeling as if I were about to pass out. That was when I spotted a pair of gleaming eyes watching us.

I clutched Laura's arm. "Someone's there," I yelped, pointing.

Laura stared. "I don't see anything."

Just then the figure stepped out of the shadows. I let out a sigh of relief. I was too far away to see his face clearly, but I recognized Will Fowler.

"Will?" I called. "What are you doing here?"

He mouthed something like, "Just came to see if you're all right."

"We're fine," I shouted back. I turned to Laura. "Aren't we?"

But Laura's face was as white as a sheet. "Amanda." Her fingers dug into my arm. "Who are you talking to?"

"Will, of course. You know, Will Fowler."

"Amanda, I think you're in shock or something," Laura said anxiously. "There's no one there."

I stared at her, then back at where Will was standing. Laura was right. Only the lilac bushes were there, faintly moving in the breeze.

I gulped. *Could I have seen Will just because I wanted*

to? My stomach tightened. It didn't seem possible, but then nothing that had happened lately seemed possible. I bent down next to Jeff. "Jeff, didn't you see him? You know, our neighbor?"

"I didn't see anyone," Jeff insisted. "There wasn't anyone there." But his voice sounded high and squeaky, the way it did the rare times he tried to lie.

"Come on, Jeff, I know you saw him."

"I didn't! I didn't!" Jeff looked like he was about to cry.

I turned to Laura. "But I saw him. I'm sure I did."

Laura studied me. "Maybe you did," she said. "But it's not that unusual to see things that aren't there when you've had a big shock."

"Perhaps you're right," I said. Just as I started walking again, I heard a sound behind me. I turned around and saw headlights coming up the driveway fast.

"Oh, brother," moaned Jeff.

" 'Oh, brother' is right," I said.

It was Mom and Dad. They were home.

Chapter 16

"**K**ids, what are you doing out here?" my dad boomed as he stepped out of the car.

"What's going on?" my mom piped up behind him. Even though my parents sounded angry, I was relieved to see them. *Maybe if I tell them what's happening, they'll keep us safe,* I thought wildly. But then I looked at their faces and knew I couldn't tell them. They would never believe it, for one thing. And for another, it would make them feel even worse than they already did about moving us here.

"Nothing. We were just . . . " I faltered.

"Looking at the stars!" Laura blurted out.

"You were what?" my mom said sternly.

"Looking at the stars," Laura repeated. "It's such a perfect night for them. And Jeff was so curious about the constellations that . . . uh . . . well, I suggested we come out here and look at them. I didn't mean to cause any trouble, Mr. and Mrs. Ryland."

I felt like laughing. Laura might not be a born spiritualist, but she was a born actress. If you heard her, you'd never dream we hadn't been out stargazing, but instead had just gone through the most terrifying experience of our lives.

"Oh, do you know the constellations?" Mom asked, the corners of her mouth turning up. I relaxed. Mom was in a great mood. Mrs. Cooper must have given her some really good recipes for her cookbook.

"Sure I do," Laura replied proudly. She pointed up at the shimmering sky. "There's Taurus, and that's Pegasus, and the Big Dipper is over there."

"Wow," Dad said as we all gazed up at the vast, starlit space overhead. "Well, I don't usually like you kids being out after dark," he added sternly. "But this is the country, after all. And I'd much rather see you stargazing, Jeff, than watching all those monster movies!"

"Yeah, it's totally cool," Jeff said. I glanced at my brother in surprise. He was doing a pretty good job of acting, too.

"Mmmm, I just love the fresh night air," Mom sighed, taking a deep breath. Then her eyes widened. "Dan, it smells like something's burning!" she cried.

Dad sniffed. "You're right!"

I froze. *What if they looked in the barn?* "It's just wood smoke," I babbled. "A lot of people in the valley heat their homes with wood stoves."

"That's what we use!" Laura exclaimed.

"Oh. I guess I'm just not used to it yet," Mom murmured. "Well, let's get in the house." She smiled at Jeff. "It's way past your bedtime, Monkey."

"Don't call me that!" Jeff protested.

We strolled into the house. Fortunately, Mom and Dad didn't notice we all had bare feet.

"Do you girls want some cocoa before bed?" Mom offered.

"No, that's okay," I said quickly.

"Yeah, we're pretty tired," Laura echoed.

We ran up the stairs to my room. My computer was still on, but there were no new messages on it. I was relieved. I didn't want to hear from any more ghosts tonight. Yet I also felt disappointed. I switched off the computer.

"I guess I should be glad nothing worse happened," I whispered to Laura. "But I'm not!"

I shuddered, recalling the look on Jeff's face as he leaned over the burning hay bale. "What if my brother sets fire to something else? What if . . . ?" my voice trailed off. *What if Tom Ryland's ghost takes him over for good? What if Rachel's ghost takes over me?* I was thinking, but I couldn't bring myself to say so out loud.

"I guess what I'm trying to say is, we don't know any more than we did when we started," I finished, close to tears.

Laura looked at me. "We do know one thing," she said.

I blinked hard. "What?"

"I know you have the talent for speaking to the spirits," Laura said solemnly. "You got Rachel's ghost to talk to you. I've never managed to get any spirit to talk to me."

"All that happened was my computer turned on," I said.

"Or you turned it on, with your mind!"

I shook my head. "I don't know, Laura. I guess I don't understand all this stuff. Maybe there's just something wrong with my computer. Why would a bunch of ghosts use the Internet to communicate, anyway?"

"Because it's a web!" Laura said. "A web of human beings communicating. Maybe the ghosts can speak on the Internet because they need human energy, and using the Net, they can channel the energy of the minds of all the people on the computer Web."

"Maybe," I agreed grudgingly. "But I still don't see how that proves I have the gift of talking to spirits."

"It doesn't," said Laura intensely. "But I just know you do. I could feel it when we were sitting at the table. There was an energy coming from you that felt just like Grandma May!"

"Great," I replied. "So how does that help us?"

"Well, it means we can talk to Rachel's ghost and maybe the other ghosts again," Laura explained.

"But I don't want to talk to any ghosts," I yelped. "I just want to know how to get rid of them—especially Tom," I added with a shudder as the image of the goblin smirking at me through the flames came into my mind.

"We also learned something else," Laura continued calmly. "Remember what Rachel said on the message? If you want to stop what's happening, Amanda, you have to find out the truth."

"I already know the truth," I muttered hopelessly. "Rachel's little brother was crazy and so is his ghost."

I pulled on my nightgown and crawled into my old sleeping bag. Laura was using my bed, and I was sleeping on the floor.

I peered around the room. "All I know is I'm going to have to watch Jeff like a hawk," I said. "Or get him exorcised. Didn't your grandmother tell you how to save someone possessed by a ghost?"

Laura sighed. "No, Amanda, I'm sorry, she didn't. But I know Grandma claimed the only way to stop a haunting was to figure out what the ghost wanted."

I was silent for a long time. "How can I figure out what a crazy boy wants?" I asked at last.

Laura didn't answer.

"Laura?" I said. Then I heard her breathing change. I peeked up at her. She was fast asleep.

I switched off the lamp and huddled in my sleeping bag. I could hear my parents moving around in their room. *They're both right next door,* I told myself. *They won't let anything bad happen.* But inside I didn't believe it. Bad things were happening, things my mom and dad could never imagine.

Pulling my sleeping bag up around my chin, I replayed in my mind what had happened in the barn. Seeing Jeff over the burning bale of hay had been strange enough, but how could I explain the way the whole world had suddenly changed, as if I had slipped into another time? Was it Rachel's ghost taking over my body, or something else, something inside me? Could Laura be right about my having a talent for talking to spirits? I hoped she wasn't, but if she was, then I had to figure out how to use it to put a stop to the ghost of Tom Ryland before it was too late!

Chapter 17

"**A**re you sure you don't want another pancake, Amanda?" my mom asked.

"No, thanks," I mumbled.

"But you've hardly eaten anything!" said my dad. "Your brother's put away twice as many pancakes as you."

"So that's unusual?" I said. "Honest, I'm just not hungry."

I wasn't, either, even though Dad had made us his extra-special blueberry-banana pancakes. My stomach felt too jittery to eat. Laura's dad had just called. He needed her to go with him to town to do some shopping. Mom and Dad had some shopping to do in town, too, so they offered to give Laura a ride. They were going to bring Jeff and me along, but Jeff had refused, saying he wasn't feeling well. Mom had given him a quick once-over. "You do look sort of pale," she agreed. "Okay, we'll go alone and Amanda will stay here with you. You won't mind, will you, sweetheart?"

The truth was, I did mind. A lot.

I pushed my plate away. "Jeff, are you sure you don't want to go into town?" I said pleadingly. "I really want to do some exploring."

"Look, I don't want to go anywhere, okay?" Jeff repeated.

"Amanda, he's obviously not feeling well," Mom said. "Don't push him. You'll get lots of other chances to go to town."

"But I was hoping—" said Laura.

"Amanda, I really don't want Jeff to get all tired out." Mom's eyes met mine.

"All right, I'll stay home with him," I said.

I sat there rigidly while my dad went outside to start the car. *If only I could tell my parents the truth, they'd understand why I don't want to stay here alone with Jeff,* I thought. But I couldn't tell them. I just couldn't.

"Come help me get my stuff," Laura said.

I followed her up the stairs.

"I'm sorry," Laura murmured helplessly when we reached my room.

I shrugged. "I'm probably just getting paranoid. This is my house. I mean, I can't go around being scared of being alone in my own home, right?"

"Right," Laura said as she hoisted her backpack over her shoulder, but she didn't sound like she meant it. "Well, I won't be gone that long, and as soon as I get home this afternoon, I'll call you on the Net, okay?"

"Okay."

We went back downstairs, and I walked her out to the car. Jeff was in the living room watching television again. He wasn't usually allowed to watch TV during the day, but Mom had said that since he was feeling sick, it was okay. I went and sat down on the couch beside him.

"There's an awesome movie on," Jeff announced, his eyes fixed on the TV screen. "It's called *Swamp Thing*."

"Swamp Thing?" I repeated sarcastically. "Wow.

Sounds great. Don't you ever do anything but watch dumb monster movies anymore?" Then I felt ashamed of myself. My brother looked so small and scared sitting there. I wondered how much, if anything, he remembered of the night before.

"Jeff, I'm sorry. I didn't mean that," I continued in a softer tone. "Listen, do you remember what happened last night? When you went to the barn?"

"I don't want to talk about it!" Jeff practically shouted. "I told you, I don't remember. I must have been sleepwalking or something."

"But—"

"Please, please just leave me alone!"

I eyed my brother helplessly. No wonder Mom was worried about him. He did look like he was getting sick. His face was so pale it was almost transparent. *He looks like he's coming down with a cold,* I thought, *but it's something worse. He's being taken over by a ghost. And so am I.*

I lifted my head. The portrait of Great-Aunt Libby stared down at me from above the fireplace. Today, she didn't look nice and friendly. She looked—anxious. I shook my head. *Portraits don't change!* I told myself. *Amanda, you are totally losing it! Get a grip.* I stretched out my hands. They were trembling like two leaves. I tried to hold them steady, but I couldn't. I stared at the TV.

What's the worst that could happen if Jeff and I just sit here and watch the movie until Mom and Dad come home? I thought. I knew I should stay with Jeff, but I couldn't bring myself to watch a movie about a monster.

"I'm going up to my room," I said. "I'll be there if you need me."

Jeff's eyes widened for a moment, then he slowly nodded. "Okay," he said.

As I ran up the stairs, I thought of what Laura had told me: *Remember what Rachel said? If you want to stop what's happening, Amanda, you have to find out the truth.*

But what did that mean? We knew the truth, didn't we?

I flopped down on my bed. Suddenly I thought of something. Laura had said the county records for Haneytown were stored on computer. That meant I could probably access them through the Internet. Maybe I could learn more about the fire that way. Anything was worth a try.

After fifteen minutes of hunting, I found the Web site I needed: *ccc.hwp.com.haneyrec*. There were thousands of pages of records—court cases, births, deaths, and real estate records on every property in the valley.

I typed in *Ryland* and waited to see what the computer would call up. Moments later, a document started scrolling across the screen. I quickly read it over, then I sighed. The document was no help at all. It was just an old deed for the Ryland farm. Then I noticed that the date on the deed was November 1931, only seven months before the fire.

"But I thought Rylands had lived in this valley for hundreds of years," I murmured aloud. I studied the deed more closely. It said that Arthur Ryland had purchased the property from the Haneytown Savings and Loan and had moved his family there from an address in town. A note at the bottom of the deed declared that the property had originally belonged to a James Fowler, who had lost it because of failure to pay taxes on the property.

I squinted at the name. *James Fowler.* It had to be the same family. Will Fowler's great-grandfather. I caught my breath, thinking of the dismal shack by the highway my father had pointed out to me the day we moved in. The Fowler place.

It must have been awful for James Fowler's family, I thought, *moving to a little shack by the side of the road after they'd owned a whole farm.* I sucked in my breath. My mind started racing. Suddenly a lot of things I hadn't understood made sense, like why Jed Fowler had hinted on the playground that day that Rylands and Fowlers didn't get along. Will had never said anything like that, though. He'd always acted like he wanted to be friends.

I frowned, thinking hard.

No wonder Will had seemed to know so much about our property! In a way, it should have been his. I typed in *Fowler* and scrolled hastily through reproductions of a number of old documents. I learned that the Fowlers had built the house we lived in and lived there for sixty years until James Fowler lost the land to the bank.

I shook my head. This information was all interesting, but what did it have to do with Jeff, me, Rachel, and Tom Ryland? Unless . . . Rachel's words pounded through my brain: *Find out the truth.* The truth was that the house had burned seven months after the Rylands had moved in—not much time at all—and what's more, the entire family had died.

Maybe it had something to do with a feud between the Rylands and the Fowlers, I thought. Then I sighed. The only problem with that idea was that witnesses had seen Tom Ryland setting fires two months before the blaze.

I shook my head again. None of it made sense.

"Hey, Amanda," Jeff called.

"What?"

"Can I get a soda?"

"Okay, but just one," I shouted back.

I stared at the computer again. An e-mail waiting sign was flashing on the upper left-hand corner of the screen. I clicked my mouse to retrieve it.

Missing, said the message. *Amanda Ryland, age twelve. Used to live in New York City . . .*

My heart began thudding. Was this another message from a ghost?

Chapter 18

I didn't want to read further, but I couldn't help myself. *Last seen: somewhere in New Hampshire*, I read aloud. *Likes: bananas, clothes (especially minidresses), cute boys, her mom's cooking . . .* I glanced up at the return address. *RealGirl* and *Madeline*. A grin slid across my face. This was no ghost talking. It was my friends, Tara and Marriane! Feeling better than I had in days, I clicked my way into the *Superstars* chat room.

Hey! I typed in. *How are you guys?*

Where have you been, Banana? Tara typed back. *We've been trying and trying to get in touch with you, but the computer keeps acting funny, or else you're not around.*

So did your dad finally manage to hook you up right? Marriane put in.

Why haven't you contacted us? Tara demanded. *Have you made so many new friends that you don't need us anymore?*

No way. I have made one friend, though. I told them about Laura. *I also met this boy who lives close by,* I added. *He was supposed to take me for a hike this weekend, but—*

Whoooo! Marriane interrupted.

But what? Tara wrote.

I hesitated. How could I tell my friends what had been going on without their thinking I'd gone crazy? On the other hand, they were my best, oldest friends. If they didn't believe me, who would? *It's a long story,* I began, and as quickly as I could, I sketched out everything that had happened. I expected my friends to be skeptical, but I was surprised.

That's weird, Tara said.

Yeah, added Marriane. *Tara, do you want to tell her or should I?*

TELL ME WHAT? I wrote back in all capital letters.

Tara replied, *A couple of times when Marriane and I tried to get in touch with you, we got these strange messages. They kept saying you were in danger, and stuff about matches and fire.*

My heart jumped into my throat.

You guys aren't joking, are you?

Would we joke about something like that? Marriane retorted. *At first, we thought it was someone playing a mean prank, because whenever they left a message, the return address was just a bunch of letters and symbols.*

We actually thought it was Mouse, Tara cut in. *But when he said it wasn't, we couldn't figure out what was going on.*

We got pretty freaked out, said Marriane.

Finally, I asked who was writing, Tara added. *The person said her name was Rachel. Does that mean anything to you?*

My hands began shaking, but I typed back, *Yes! Rachel is the name of the girl who died in the fire!*

Are you serious? Tara said. *What are we going to do?*

The fact that she said *we* made me feel a lot better.

I don't know, I started to type when I heard a ringing noise. I was so startled, I jumped to my feet, but it was only the doorbell.

"Jeff?" I shouted.

"Amanda, get down here right now!"

"Coming!" I leaned over and quickly typed, *Got to go. Be back soon.*

Then I sped downstairs. I almost bumped into Jeff, who was running up. The moment I saw him, I knew something was very wrong.

"Jeff, what is it?" I cried. My little brother's eyes had that funny, faraway look again. But there was something else I hadn't seen before: A look of terror.

He licked his lips and said in a voice so faint I could hardly hear it, "It's him. He's come back."

"Who's come back?" I gasped. "Tom?"

But Jeff didn't answer. The ringing at the door was getting louder and more insistent.

"Go upstairs," I commanded. "Go upstairs and go into my room and shut the door. Tara and Marriane are on-line. Tell them we're in trouble!" Jeff nodded and ran. I wondered if I was crazy, if I was totally overreacting. There was only one way to find out. Cautiously, I took a step down the staircase. The front door had a smoky-colored glass window in it, and through it I saw a head of blond hair.

I knew at once who it was.

Will Fowler.

Chapter 19

"Amanda, is that you? Remember I said I was coming over? Don't you want to go on the hike?" Will called.

I took another step down the stairs. *Relax,* I told myself. *It's just Will. There's nothing to be scared of.* But I kept thinking of the terror in my brother's eyes. My mind began to race. If Arthur Ryland had taken over the Fowler farm, maybe the Fowlers had been angry enough to get revenge! I paused at the bottom of the stairs.

"Amanda, aren't you going to let me in?" Will's voice sounded ordinary but confused about what was going on. Yet still I hesitated.

What if he was the one who set the fires? I thought crazily. *What if he did it and Tom was blamed?*

Then I shook my head, feeling dizzy. What was I thinking about? Tom Ryland had been dead for sixty-five years. Will Fowler hadn't even been born at the time of the fire. But something was making me uneasy. Something Will had said. Then I realized what it was. The first time I met her, Laura had told me that Will Fowler and his family had just moved back to the valley after being away for years. But Will had said he had lived here all his life. If he'd lied about that, what else had he lied about?

"Amanda, come on!" Will's voice sounded impatient now. "Open the door!" It was not a request, it was a command.

"I don't think I can go on that hike today, Will," I called faintly. "My brother has chicken pox—"

"You're lying," Will said. "Tom had chicken pox last year!"

I felt as if the floor were sliding out from under me. I grabbed the banister and steadied myself. My heart was beating hard, as if it had a life of its own.

"Tom?" I said faintly. "But Tom doesn't live here. Tom's been dead for sixty-five years!"

I could see Will's head moving behind the thick glass, and terror rose in my throat. "Just go away!" I shouted. "Please, please just go away!"

I heard the doorknob rattling. I took a step backward, then I let out a gasp. Will's face was getting clearer and clearer. I could see his eyes gleaming, boring into mine. But they weren't green anymore—now they were yellow. I felt a chill of fear as I realized that they looked exactly like the eyes of the creature from my dream. I stepped back again, but still the eyes came closer. I couldn't believe what I was seeing. Will was walking through the door. He was inside the house. He had passed right through the locked door!

Chapter 20

I stared at him, shocked. I had seen him walk through the door just like a shadow, but now he looked as solid as any normal fourteen-year-old boy. But he wasn't—he was a ghost. I scrambled backward up the stairs.

"Who are you?" I whispered. "You're not Will Fowler!"

"Oh, but I am," Will replied. He smiled a strange, sad-looking smile. "My name is William Fowler, only most people don't call me Will. They call me Billy."

I felt like I'd just been shoved into an ice-cold shower.

"Billy," I repeated, remembering my brother's words on the playground. *It wasn't me. It was Billy.* And I remembered, as well, one of the messages I'd received from the ghosts.

Beware Tom, Rachel. Beware Billy!

I'd assumed the message meant beware of Tom. But I'd been wrong. The ghosts were telling me to beware of Billy!

I took another step backward, my heart sinking. I longed to turn around and run, but I knew it wouldn't do any good. Billy wasn't alive. He was a ghost. He could pass through locked doors. He could probably do anything he wanted to, even set fires. I shuddered, watching him. He appeared almost transparent again, the outlines of his body shimmering with an eerie, pale light, his yellow eyes gleaming faintly in the dim hallway. I couldn't believe I'd never noticed before how cold and calculating his eyes were.

"You set those fires, didn't you?" I shouted. "You set them and blamed Tom for them. How could you do it, Billy?"

Billy's mouth curved up. "It was easy. Tom was such a scaredy-cat. I got him to help me set the first one, and I told him if he ever told anyone what we'd done or that I'd been there, I'd push him down the old well by the house. He was so scared that even when I set more fires, he didn't tell anyone. I think Rachel figured it out, though."

A look of regret flickered in his eyes. "I liked Rachel," he said almost mournfully. "We were friends once. She said she would never forgive me. She said she would tell. That's why I had to hurry."

"Hurry?" I repeated in a hollow voice.

"Yes. I had to hurry and set the place on fire." Billy's voice was flat and dead-sounding.

I shuddered, thinking of the burned staircase—and of Rachel, Tom, and their parents trying to escape from a house engulfed in flames.

"But why, Billy?" I asked. "Why did you do it?"

All of a sudden, the expression on Billy's face changed. He no longer looked cruel and cold. Instead, he looked like a scared kid. "Dad made me." The words were just a whisper. "He said I couldn't be in the family unless I got those folks off our land. He locked me in the cellar and wouldn't give me supper until I said I would.

"It was supposed to work out fine," he continued.

"My daddy had some money hidden away, and when your folks were gone, driven off by the fire, he was going to buy this place back. Only it didn't happen that way. I didn't mean for them to get trapped." His voice rose. "I never meant it, and I . . . I ran down the wrong staircase, the back one. I didn't know it was going to burn like that. The floor fell away, and I fell down the well shaft. I tried and tried to climb out, but I couldn't."

So that was why they'd never found his body! It had fallen down the well shaft below the house.

"So why didn't your father buy the place back?"

"I don't know. All I know is, you are still here." Billy squared his shoulders and moved toward me. I backed away and started up the stairs.

"It's over, Billy," I called. "It all happened a long time ago. What do you want with me and my brother?"

Billy's eyes flashed, and he murmured something so softly that at first I wasn't sure I'd heard him. "I want," he said, "to make it turn out right."

For a moment, I didn't know what he meant.

And then I saw the matches in his hand and I understood.

"I failed Daddy. He would never forgive me. I knew he would never forgive me. I've been alone all this time. Not part of the family!" Billy's ghost cried. "But I know what to do. I'm going to burn this place to the ground and get rid of you people. Then this can be Fowler land again."

I stared at him in horror. Then I turned and ran.

Chapter 21

I raced into my room and slammed the door behind me. Jeff was sitting on my bed. His eyes looked enormous in his small, pale face. "Did you tell Tara and Marriane?" I gasped.

My brother shook his head. "There's something wrong with the computer. No one's there," he sobbed.

I leaned over the keyboard. The computer was on, but the screen was blank. Frantically I punched keys, but nothing happened.

"Wait here," I ordered Jeff. I slipped out to the hall and picked up the phone by my parents' room. The line was dead. I could hear the wind gusting around the windows and, behind it, silence. In the silence I could sense Billy's presence. He was moving through the house, plotting, planning. I ran back into my room and closed the door.

"He's here, isn't he?" Jeff asked in a hollow voice.

"What do you know about him, Jeff?" I fixed my eyes on my little brother's face. "Please tell me. It's important."

"He came to see me," Jeff stammered. "He was at school. He gave me the matches and told me to light one. He said it would be neat. I'd be surprised. And then . . . then the grass was burning and I was in big trouble, but . . . I didn't mean to do anything, Amanda. I didn't, honest!"

"It's okay," I said softly.

"He said if I told, the same thing that happened to Tom Ryland would happen to me. I thought if I went along, I could save us. But he's never going to let us out of here," Jeff wailed, the tears coming faster. "It's like Tom. Tom was scared of him, too, and he didn't tell, and he died!"

"Jeff, I won't let him hurt you," I said.

My brother just looked at me hopelessly.

I jumped as the door to my room creaked, but it didn't open. I watched it carefully. A pale shape like a wisp of dust slowly twisted into the room through the door. It blew over toward my brother. For a moment, I thought I saw Billy. I let out a strangled cry. "Jeff?" I said. My little brother rose to his feet and started walking toward me.

"Jeff?" I said again. My little brother's face was expressionless, and his eyes were staring straight ahead. "Jeff, stop it!" I shouted, but he kept moving toward me. Then I saw his eyes. They weren't his eyes—blue and friendly. Instead, they were yellow and cold—ghoulish eyes, Billy's eyes!

I remembered something Laura had told me her Grandma May had said. *Most ghosts can't act or speak on their own. They need the energy of living people to help them.* I suddenly noticed Jeff's hand was closed around a pack of matches.

"Jeff, no!" I screamed at the top of my lungs.

But my brother pushed me aside. He was much stronger than he normally was. He was as strong as a fourteen-year-old boy.

Whap! I landed on the floor.

When I looked up again, Jeff was gone.

I tore through the house, calling his name, but he was nowhere to be found. Then I remembered the secret door to the other part of the attic. I ran downstairs to the kitchen, squeezed myself behind the refrigerator, and pushed it as hard as I could. It was no use. The door was locked from the inside!

I went to the front door, but I couldn't open it, either. I was alone in the house with the ghost of Billy Fowler. I was locked in, and any minute the house was going to start burning.

I could break a window and get help, I thought, but I knew I would never be back in time. What was more, I could never leave my brother alone in the house with a murderous ghost.

"Jeff! Jeff! Where are you?" I shouted.

"Amanda!" I heard a faint cry coming from the attic. I pushed and kicked at the door with every ounce of my strength, but it wouldn't budge.

"Amanda!" Jeff wailed. His cry faded, and in its place I heard insane, mocking laughter. And then I heard another voice. It wasn't Billy this time. It was a voice that sounded almost like Jeff's, but wasn't.

"Rachel, I'm sorry! It's too late!" sobbed the voice of Tom Ryland. "Too late, too late . . ."

Chapter 22

With the echo of Tom Ryland's ghostly voice in my ears, I banged on the solid oak door desperately for what felt like hours. I didn't have a prayer of breaking it down.

Laura's voice suddenly echoed in my mind.

You have the talent of speaking with the spirit world, she was saying. *If you want to talk to the ghosts again, you can.* In a flash it came to me. I remembered Laura saying: *Maybe the ghosts can speak on the Internet because they need human energy, and using the Net, they can channel the energy of the minds of all the people on the computer Web.* That was the answer! I had to get in touch with Rachel and Tom and the others on Ghostweb. I had to get them to help me. It was my only chance. But could I do it?

I turned and raced up the stairs. The house seemed silent again, but I could feel Billy's mind, searching for me, wondering what I was thinking. I burst into my room and ran over to my computer. The screen was still blank, but the cursor was blinking. I sat down and put my hands on the keyboard.

Try to see a door, a door into the other world, Laura's voice said in my head. *Open your mind and ask the ghosts to come in.*

I took a deep breath. I tried with all my might to envision an open door, but the only door I could see was the secret door in the kitchen. The locked door with my brother behind it.

I screwed my eyes up tighter. The door was still closed, but a light was glowing around it now—not an orange light like the light of a fire, but a soft, white light, like the glow of a full moon. Slowly, slowly, the door swung open, and there was a figure I recognized: Rachel. Her eyes were large and luminous, and they bored into mine. Then her mouth moved.

"Amanda, we want to come, but we need help. Get help!" she breathed.

What did she mean? Then I recalled what Laura had told me. Evil ghosts are trapped in this world, but good ghosts need help getting back here. *They need minds willing to call them back to earth, to let them cross over from the spirit world.* Rachel was telling me the ghosts needed more people, more living human energy.

But how was I supposed to get more people to help me?

I opened my eyes and stared at the screen. A message was flashing at me.

Amanda, what's going on? it said.

I let out a deep, shuddering breath. It was Tara. Tara and Marriane! I was back in our chat room. I put my fingers on the keys and began typing.

The ghost has Jeff, I wrote. *No time to explain. I need you to help me call up the other ghosts.*

What? Marriane typed.

I couldn't blame her for being confused. It was a lot to take in all at once. But I didn't know how to explain it better, and I had no time to spare.

How? Tara wrote.

I'll tell you how, blinked a message signed *Lorelei*.

My spirits soared. It was Laura, and she was just in the nick of time.

Chapter 23

Put your hands on the keyboard and make your minds totally blank, Laura wrote. *Then try to imagine an open door. A door to the other world . . .*

Goose bumps rose on my arms as Laura typed on. I wondered where Jeff was now and what was happening to him. I took my fingers from the keyboard. *Hurry!* I mouthed at the screen. *Please hurry!*

Amanda, Tara, Marriane, focus on the door! Laura commanded over the Net.

I closed my eyes and focused. This time the door was much clearer. It was surrounded by a shimmery light. I could almost feel the energy coming from it. The light was no longer pale, but a deep brilliant yellow, and the door looked like it was about to burst open.

I breathed in deeply, gasped, and opened my eyes.

I could hear a faint crackling noise above my head, and I smelled a smell that was all too familiar. Smoke!

I let out a cry and closed my eyes again. My heart skipped a beat. The door in my mind was wide open now. I could see it etched behind my eyeballs so vividly that it looked real. Pale figures were streaming through it, figures surrounded by shining, brilliant light. Their faces weren't hideous like the monster in my dream, or terrifying as Billy's had been when he came through our front door. These faces were kind and smiling.

I opened my eyes again and stared in wonder.

I had to be imagining it, but I wasn't! Pale shapes were twisting out of my computer screen. More and more of them came. I could dimly make out faces and the shapes of arms and legs and long, flowing robes.

"What in the world—?" I cried. Suddenly I felt a hand take hold of mine. A voice whispered in my ear, "Amanda, hurry! Before it's too late!"

Chapter 24

I gazed up. Rachel was beside me. Her eyes were blazing so brightly that they looked like they were on fire, and her mouth was set in a determined line. "Come," she said.

I felt myself being lifted into the air and pulled out of my room and down the hall. A surge of hope passed through me as we reached the top of the stairs. I was being led toward the secret door. This time, with Rachel's help, I felt sure I would be able to open it. As we moved down the stairs, I began to smell the burning more strongly. The house was filling up with thick, bluish smoke. In terror, I glanced at Rachel, whose ghostly hand was gripping mine, but she stared straight ahead.

The next thing I knew, we had reached the secret door. I gaped at it in horror. It was the door in my dream, the door surrounded by thick, burning flames!

I went totally rigid. "Jeff!" I shouted.

I thought I could hear my brother shrieking, but it was hard to tell above the crackling of the flames. Suddenly, behind me, I heard insane, high-pitched laughter. I whirled around.

Billy was standing in the center of the kitchen. He

was in flames, too. My heart jumped into my throat. He still looked like a boy, but his burning skin and blazing yellow eyes reminded me again of the creature from my dream!

A scream froze in my throat as he raised his arms and started toward me. I felt Rachel's hand squeeze mine. I glanced over at her. Her eyes were no longer shining. They looked dull and lifeless. She gazed at me with a look of infinite sorrow, and my stomach turned over.

"It's too late, isn't it?" I said hopelessly.

Rachel shook her head. "No, but you must be brave," she answered. She gestured toward the burning door. "Go!"

"But how can I go in there?" I whimpered.

She didn't say a word, but it was as if I heard her voice inside me. *If you are brave I will help you, but you must act.*

I turned to face the door. Flames were leaping out of it now, licking the walls and the ceiling, spreading columns of thick, black smoke across the kitchen, clouding the windows. Even though it was the middle of the afternoon, it looked like the deepest part of the night. I hesitated only a moment, then, closing my eyes, I raced forward through the door of flames.

I steeled myself to feel the burning heat of the fire and intense pain, but to my astonishment I felt nothing. Instead, it was as if I were floating. I glanced around for Rachel, but she was nowhere in sight.

"You can't leave me now!" I sobbed as I struggled up the stairs through the smoke and flames.

It's all right, I'm here, I heard a voice inside me say.

"What do you mean? Where are you?" I cried.

Just keep going, the voice said.

The flames were all around me now, so close I could not understand why I wasn't burning up.

I glanced down at myself. My dress looked like it was on fire, yet still I felt nothing. A jolt of fear passed through me.

Maybe I feel nothing because I'm already dead, I thought dully. *Maybe I'm dead and so is Jeff and this is all just a dream.*

Stretching my hands out in front of me, I kept going. I was at the top of the attic staircase now. I peered around, trying to see Jeff through all the smoke.

"Jeff, where are you?" I wept.

A figure materialized ahead of me. It was an old woman with long, white hair. She was wearing a faded print dress. I gazed at her incredulously. "Great-Aunt Libby?" I breathed. She looked exactly like her portrait in the living room.

"He's over here, honey," she said, pointing.

I saw a crumpled figure lying in the corner.

"Jeff!" I gasped.

"I'm afraid he's only semiconscious. You'll have to carry him down," whispered Great-Aunt Libby. "And hurry," she added, her voice wavering. "We're protecting you from the flames for the moment, but we can't keep a shield around you much longer. Rachel's doing her best to hold Billy back, but he's stronger than the rest of us. He'll try to stop you from ever getting out."

I nodded and ran over to my brother. Jeff's eyelids were fluttering, and he was breathing shallowly. I hoisted him up into my arms and struggled to the top of the stairs. "Amanda?" he muttered.

"It's okay," I said.

I was about to start down the stairs when a black

form emerged out of the smoke. It was Billy. He had grown to an enormous size.

"Where do you think you're going?" he growled, grinning evilly. His huge, flaming hand gripped me by the shoulder. It was like my dream, when a hand held me down as the house burned—only this time it was real!

Chapter 25

The smoke was getting thicker. I could only dimly make out Billy's face, growing ever more distorted by the flames. He looked less and less like a person and more and more like a monster. I began to cough. Suddenly I could feel the heat, the terrible heat all around.

So this was what Great-Aunt Libby meant when she said the ghosts couldn't keep a shield around us much longer, I thought hopelessly. *The shield must already be getting weaker.*

The heat was growing more and more intense. Billy's hand was burning into my shoulder. "Let me go," I pleaded, knowing that if Jeff and I didn't get out of there soon, we never would.

"Please Will—I mean, Billy—please let us go!" I looked up at him. "I thought we were friends."

Billy's eyes flashed. "No. You only want to take my place. You only want to get rid of me."

"No! I never wanted to get rid of you," I said desperately. "That was just your crazy father. Rachel never wanted to get rid of you, either. Neither did Tom or any of the Rylands. Your dad lost the farm to the bank. It wasn't my family's fault! When they bought it, they didn't know how you all felt!"

"But Dad said—" A look of confusion came into Billy's eyes, and for a moment his features were once again like those of a boy. "Dad said your dad stole it from him!"

"That's a lie!" The voice came from me, but it wasn't mine. It was Rachel's. In a flash I understood what she'd meant when she said she was still with me. She was inside me, part of me! "Your dad gambled the farm away. Don't you remember, Billy? How he'd go to town every weekend and how your mom wou d cry? Don't you remember how all winter you used to come to our house because there was nothing at your house to eat? Don't you remember how you used to be my friend, Billy? How you were Tom's friend? Don't you?"

Billy's face crumbled. I blinked. He didn't look like a monster now. He looked scared and sad. I could even see tears gleaming in his eyes.

"I never meant for anyone to die," he whispered. "Now I can't come back, but I can't rest, either. Rachel, you have to help me!"

"How can I help you when you keep doing wrong?" Rachel asked, her voice rising out of my throat. "I can only help you find rest if you put a stop to this. If you let these people go and clear Tom's name."

Billy Fowler shook his head. "I don't know if I can."

I stared at him. His form seemed to be growing lighter, almost transparent. Then I saw a dark, hulking shape appear beside him. "Billy!" a voice hissed. A twisted face formed itself out of the rising smoke. My blood turned to ice. I had seen this face before. Billy's face had only reminded me of the creature in my dream, but this was really it—the nightmare come to life!

"Dad!" Billy's voice was a choked whisper.

I gazed in horror at the green skin and leering

features. This was the spirit of James Fowler, Billy's father. Grandma May had been right when she said that the spirits of people who did bad things on earth didn't even look human. The figure in front of me looked like some repulsive gargoyle brought to life.

"Billy," Mr. Fowler's ghost rasped. "Billy, you have to do what I told you. You have to do it for the family. Go on, do like I told you, son."

His yellow eyes glowed like hot coals burning through the darkness. Although sweat was pouring off me, inside I felt as cold as death. "Go on, Billy!" The creature's lips twisted into an evil grin. "Do what I told you. These kids are mine!"

Billy cowered as the dark shape of his father seemed to grow larger and larger, like a leaping flame. "Do it, Billy!" the harsh voice commanded.

"Billy, if you do this, you'll never find rest," I shouted frantically. Billy looked at me, then at the gnarled and contorted face of his father.

"Do it, Billy!"

"You lied to me, Dad," Billy said, his voice almost a sob. "They never stole our farm. You lost it yourself!"

"Just do like I told you!" his father hissed.

"No!" Billy cried. The two of them turned on each other, two grappling shapes twisting around each other like smoke. Then I heard a terrible cry, and both of them vanished in a burst of flame. The staircase was empty.

"Go," I heard Great-Aunt Libby say. "The shield will protect you." She gave me a shove, and with Jeff in my arms, I staggered down the staircase. I ran through the smoke-filled kitchen and out the back door.

Breathing in great sobbing gulps of cool, fresh air, I stumbled onto the grass. Then I collapsed.

Chapter 26

"**I**s she all right? Please, tell me she's all right." I heard crying. It was my mom. I struggled to open my eyes and looked up into the face of a dark-haired man I'd never seen before—a young man dressed in a fireman's uniform.

"How did the fire trucks get here?" I murmured groggily.

"The Fowlers called," the fireman replied. "You know Will Fowler who lives down the road? He saw smoke and gave us a call."

"Oh," I said weakly. I sat up.

"I told you she'd be okay, ma'am," said the fireman with a grin. "She might be suffering from shock, though. I'll get the paramedics to take another look at her." He winked at me. "That was a brave thing you did, young lady, getting your brother out of the house."

"Jeff?" I shouted. "Where is he?"

"It's okay, Amanda." My dad put his hand on my shoulder. "The paramedics are taking care of him now. He got a few burns, but apparently they're only second-degree."

"Does that mean he'll be okay?"

"The paramedics tell us he'll soon be good as new," Mom said tearfully.

My dad turned to another, older fireman, who was

winding up a long hose at the back of the truck. "So how did the fire start?" he asked.

"Near as we can figure, lightning hit the antenna up there. See how it's blasted away? I'm afraid it was a freak accident—the kind of thing that happens in only one in a million cases."

"Oh." Dad opened his mouth and shut it. "There was another fire here a long time ago."

"Oh, yeah." The fireman nodded. "I heard about that. Same part of the house, too. Well, this time you were lucky. We caught it before it damaged the structure much. Your insurance should cover the repairs."

I looked up at the house. The roof was still smoking, but the fireman was right. It didn't look as if there'd been much damage. "The place was full of flames," I muttered. I wondered how it was possible that the fire had done so little damage. Then I remembered what Great-Aunt Libby had said about the shield the spirits had put around Jeff and me. Maybe the spirits from Ghostweb had also protected the house.

I stood up and put my arms around my mom. "Oh, Mom, I was so scared!" I whispered.

Mom hugged me tight. "I'll bet. I'm so proud of you."

I spotted Jeff lying on a stretcher in the grass surrounded by paramedics. My heart in my mouth, I raced over to him.

"Jeff, are you really okay?"

"Amanda!" He looked at me and smiled. "Tom said good-bye. He said he can go away now."

"Who's Tom?" Mom asked.

"He's probably just confused," Dad told her.

But I knew my little brother was giving me a message from one of our visitors from the beyond.

I stared across the lawn. The firemen were taking down their ladders. Then I saw a light shine in my bedroom window, a flash of light like the reflection of a mirror. I squinted up at it. I could dimly see a circle of faces peering at me through the glass: a white-haired woman, a girl with wavy blonde hair, and a boy with red curls. Great-Aunt Libby, Rachel, and Tom!

"Bye," I whispered, and I lifted my hand and waved. Rachel's face broke into a smile, and then she waved her hand, too. I glanced away for a moment, and when I looked back up at the window again, there was no one there.

Chapter 27

"**I** don't think I can possibly eat another bite," I groaned.

Laura grinned at me. "Sure you can. You'll just have to buy bigger jeans," she teased. I looked at the warm strawberry-rhubarb pie Mom had just set on the table.

"Okay, okay," I grumbled. "But this is the last piece, I swear!"

Jeff stuck out his tongue at me. "Wimp! I could eat at least ten more pieces!" he crowed.

Mom rolled her eyes. "I bet you could," she said. "But this is definitely the last one."

We were sitting around our kitchen table. Mom had asked us to do an informal taste-test of recipes for strawberry-rhubarb pie. The best one would go into her cookbook, which she'd decided to call *Country Treasures.* I thought it was a corny title myself, but Mom's agent said with a name like that the book would probably sell a ton. Which was a good thing if we wanted to keep living in the country, and we did—even Jeff and me.

It had been two weeks since the fire, and Dad had almost finished repapering the old secret staircase. The man from the insurance company was amazed that the fire hadn't caused more damage. "Fires caused by lightning often behave strangely," he said, "but it's still a one-in-a-million chance that a house escapes with so little structural damage!"

If only he knew how one in a million, I thought as Mom set another warm piece of pie in front of me.

"Okay, taste this, and then you can all vote on your favorite."

"But what if we can't remember what they all taste like?" Jeff demanded. "Can we get second helpings?"

"Sure, if you want to weigh three hundred pounds when this is over," I said. Jeff pretended to slug me. Then we all dug in.

"Tender, flaky crust," Laura murmured.

"Fantastic filling!" said Jeff.

"Yeah, not too sweet or sour," I agreed.

"Honey, this is your best yet," my dad declared.

"Whose recipe is it?" Jeff wanted to know.

"Oh, umm . . . " Mom rifled through her index cards of recipes. "You'll never guess," she said quietly. "It's Great-Aunt Libby's."

I looked down at the plate, thinking of Great-Aunt Libby, her hand on my shoulder as she helped Jeff and me stand up to the ghost of Billy Fowler.

"Great-Aunt Libby was an incredible person," Jeff said.

I glanced at him. His face looked solemn and dreamy, and I realized he was remembering the same thing I was.

"She was," Dad said in a surprised voice. "But how did you reach that conclusion, Jeff?"

"Well, uh," Jeff stammered, "because, uh, she made such incredible pie!"

"So is Great-Aunt Libby's recipe the winner?" Mom asked.

"Yes!" we all chorused.

Then Laura, Jeff, and I exchanged glances.

"You know," Laura said softly, "this house really does have a nice feeling to it."

I nodded, looking around. There were still building supplies—buckets of plaster and paint—scattered all over, but Laura was right. The house *did* feel good. The creepy, watchful feeling was gone—I hoped forever.

The day after the fire, the workmen Dad had hired found Billy Fowler's bones. Billy had fallen down the old well shaft just like he'd said. He'd gotten halfway up but had never managed to escape.

When my dad called the sheriff's office, the elderly coroner who came out to examine the body said Billy must have hidden there, hoping to escape the fire. The oil-soaked rag they found clutched in Billy's skeleton's fingers meant he had probably been the one to start the blaze. "That clears up two mysteries around this place," the coroner said. Then he added softly, "You know, I knew Tom Ryland when I was a little boy, and I never figured him setting that fire."

The sheriff's office then released Billy's skeleton to his family so he could be buried in the Fowler family plot in the cemetery in town.

I peered at the open stairwell. I was glad Billy had finally been found and would be buried with the rest of his family. Maybe now he'd be at peace. Even so, thinking of him lying there at the top of the well shaft all those years gave me the creeps. Billy Fowler had been a troubled, twisted boy. His ghost had tried to murder me and my little brother. Yet, whenever I thought about him, there was sorrow mixed with my fear and my anger. With a dad like James Fowler, Billy had never had much of a chance.

I shivered and looked up to see Mom watching me.

"What's wrong, Amanda? You look as if you've seen a ghost."

"No—uh, I think I just ate too much pie," I mumbled. "Hey, Laura, you want to go up to my room for a while? I thought we could call Tara and Marriane."

"Great." Laura jumped up. "I can ask Marriane how that show was last night. You know, *Dancing Feet?*"

I grinned. As I'd expected, Laura and Marriane had quickly become best buddies. They did nothing but yak about acting! Sometimes Tara and I got bored, and I got a little jealous, but mostly I was glad. My best friends in the whole world liked my new best friend. Everything had turned out perfectly.

I moved up the stairs ahead of Laura. Halfway up I saw a familiar figure—an old lady in a faded dress.

"I'm so glad my pie won," she said happily as I walked past.

"Your pie deserved to win," I answered.

Laura looked at me. "Who are you talking to?" she asked.

I smiled. It made Laura nervous the way I was always talking to myself. Laura said her Grandma May used to do the same thing. "I never really managed to get accustomed to it," Laura had said to me. "Other people thought she was crazy!"

I could understand that, but I understood Grandma May even better. Although Laura had seen that I had a talent for talking to spirits, she didn't have a clue what it was like. Once you let the talent take root in you, it grew until you were always seeing two worlds—the world that was there and the world of the spirits. Anyone who didn't have the gift couldn't understand.

Jeff passed us on the stairs on his way up to his room. He walked by Great-Aunt Libby without giving any indication he had seen her. I had hoped Jeff would be like me and keep seeing spirits wherever he looked, but he wasn't. I had a feeling he could see them if he wanted to, but he didn't.

Maybe he was just too young.

I winked at Great-Aunt Libby and continued on to my room. I was thinking about how Mom had said I wasn't going to lose anything by moving to the country. Mom would never know how right she'd been. Not only had I not lost anything, I had gained more than I could ever have dreamed: an insight into a whole new world few people even know exists.

A few days later, I finally met the real Will Fowler. It was another foggy morning and Jeff had a bad cold, so Mom was keeping him home. Ever since the fire, both my parents had tended to fuss over him. I was walking to the bus stop and had just passed under the old oak trees where the spirit of Billy Fowler had first appeared to me. I was whistling to myself when I heard a twig crunch behind me.

I whirled around. A boy with green eyes and blond hair was walking toward me, a distant look in his glowing eyes.

A thrill of fear passed through me. "Billy?" I whispered.

"Actually, people call me Will," the boy answered. Then he looked at me harder. "You must be the Ryland girl. Amanda, right?" he said.

"Right," I giggled, but inside I felt nervous. *He looks so much like Billy, he could be Billy,* I was thinking.

"I heard you called the fire department," I said.

"Thank you. It may have saved our house."

He shrugged nervously. "It was nothing."

"That's not true!" I exclaimed. "It was pretty amazing that you saw the smoke from so far away, and on a cloudy day, too."

Will's face turned a shade lighter, and his piercing green eyes met mine. "It was kind of weird," he said. "The truth is, I didn't see the smoke exactly. I just . . . "

He didn't say more, but he didn't have to. The answer was written on his face. So Billy Fowler truly felt sorry at the end. My chest suddenly felt tight. Then Will leaned toward me. "He used to come to me a lot," he said. "I'm glad it's over."

"Not as glad as I am," I said. I took a deep breath of the morning air. I smelled lilacs, cut grass, rain—and not a hint of anything burning anywhere.

"I see a lot of things other people don't," Will added in a low voice.

I nodded. "So do I," I whispered. I felt scared, but excited, too. Here was someone else who knew what it was like to see another world.

I looked up. The yellow school bus was lurching down the road. "Oops, I have to go," I said. "See you around!"

Will nodded. He resembled his great-uncle so closely, it made me feel shivery inside. But when I looked at him more carefully, his face seemed nicer somehow.

I jumped as the old school bus stopped in front of me. "I have to go," I repeated.

Will grinned, a gentle, sheepish-looking grin. "Well, hope I see you soon, Amanda," he said. "I have a feeling we're going to be good friends."

"Me, too," I said softly as I boarded the bus.

I meant it, too. At least, I meant it until I sat down.

Laura wasn't taking the bus that morning because she had a dentist appointment before school, so I was sitting alone, next to the window. As Mrs. Perkins pressed down the accelerator and the bus jolted forward, I glanced back outside.

Will Fowler was still standing there, staring up at me. The look in his eyes made me feel ice cold all over.

His eyes were yellow and gleaming, and all around him was the faint reddish glow of a distant fire.

Then his eyes met mine and he smiled—not the sweet-looking grin he'd given me earlier, but the gloating, bitter smile of James Fowler. For a moment, his face became distorted, a monster mask. His mouth moved. I've never been good at lip-reading, but somehow I knew what he was saying.

"Rachel!"

An icy tremor passed through me. "Billy!" I gasped. The awful grin faded from Will Fowler's face, and the reddish glow vanished. He blinked up at the bus, looking confused. But I knew what I'd seen. And I knew the boy standing by the side of the road was Will Fowler and he wasn't, just like I'd been Amanda Ryland and Rachel Ryland at the same time.

Billy hadn't gone away forever after all. Nor had he broken free of his father's evil influence. I had seen the glimmer in his eyes, the cruel sneer twisting his face.

Billy was back.

Don't miss any of these exciting books!